TAMING THE BEAST

A WOLVES of WHARTON Novella
Book Three

BEAU LAKE

4 Horsemen
Publications, Inc.

4 Horsemen Publications, Inc.
1497 Main St. Suite 169
Dunedin, FL 34698
4horsemenpublications.com
info@4horsemenpublications.com

Typesetting by Michelle Cline
Editor Vanessa Valiente

Library of Congress Control Number: 2021944552

Print ISBN: 978-1-64450-333-1
Audio ISBN: 978-1-64450-331-7
Ebook ISBN: 978-1-64450-332-4

TABLE OF CONTENTS

I. 1937

PROLOGUE
(NADIA)

───────◁◆▷───────

Milton calls the thicket of trees just past the buttress dam "our's." It's a far less appealing part of the reservoir with straight-trunked trees planted in rows meant to hide the curved concrete eyesore feeding water into the lakeside. The dam is inordinately loud, providing hydroelectric power to Knox and Sevier Counties. Often, I leave our spot with a migraine, a pulsing sunspot just behind my right eye. But, every weekend, we're here, lounging on the hood of his parents' Buick.

"It's private," Milton says, as if he needs to convince me.

I'm just content to be here with him, tucked under his arm.

This afternoon, I brought a picnic lunch in a hamper: deviled eggs, watermelon, and pigs in a blanket.

Milton whoops when he peels back the lid of the repurposed margarine container, finding the glossy eggs stuffed with fluorescent yellow yolk, minced onion, and chopped ham. He takes a bite, paprika adorning his upper lip like a gingery mustache. When I point it out, he asks, "Do I look like my father?"

"No." I giggle, thinking of his father's bristly mustache, a poor facsimile of Roosevelt's walrus-like stache. "You'd need much more paprika."

Milton takes another egg from the container and pops the whole thing into his mouth. "These are yummy," he mumbles as flecks of egg fly from his full mouth. "Did your mom make them?"

"I did. I wanted today to be special. It's our anniversary, after all," I reply.

I had woken up early this morning to make our lunch, squinting at my mother's recipe cards. While they were written in precise cursive, it was difficult to understand her shorthand. Did "p" stand for pound, pinch, or something else entirely? I'm still not certain I put the requisite amount of mayonnaise in the eggs, though luckily, Milton isn't complaining.

"Is it?"

He's forgotten. A lance of disappointment edges between my ribs, and I wrap my arms around my midsection. I had thought today would be special. After all, we are weeks from graduating high school, and it's our first anniversary. Surely, he was meant to propose! Wasn't he?

I'm a silly, stupid, little girl. I blame Hannah Carmichael. She's the one who planted the seed in my head during English class, when we were supposed to be discussing Chaucer. "Nadia Fairbanks has such a nice ring to it," she'd said, smacking her gum. "It's so much easier to pronounce than Montanari."

Milton reaches for the gingham handkerchief that I had wrapped the pigs in a blanket with, oblivious to my pointed silence. Clearly, he doesn't intend to apologize for forgetting the date.

I slide off the hood, heaving a sigh.

"Where are you going?" he asks.

"I'm going for a walk," I reply over my shoulder. "I'm not hungry."

He doesn't follow me.

The reservoir is a large expanse of water, a diverted river turned into a bowl-shaped lake. It's named after some big cat that makes the manmade habitat its home, but I can't remember which. *I wish a tiger—or whatever it is—would just swallow me up. Then, perhaps, I wouldn't have to feel so humiliated.*

I find a floating dock a half-mile down the shoreline, clearly jerry-rigged by teenagers. It's made of fifty-five-gallon barrels, lashed together with mismatched plywood haphazardly placed on top. It's anchored to shore by a long nylon rope, tied around a massive tree.

I take off my heels and climb aboard the bobbing eyesore, putting my feet into the chilly water. Closing my eyes, I turn my face up toward the sun.

Suddenly, a branch snaps behind me.

"Milton?" I call, craning my head in the direction of the noise.

But there's no one there. I turn back toward the water, watching tiny, dark-colored tadpoles swim around my bare feet. Then, I hear a low-pitched growl. Before I can turn around and look, the floating dock bucks violently beneath me. I manage to grab one of the cords holding the dock together before I can be flung off; the rope burns my hands.

Despite the fearsome growl, I expect to see Milton on the shore, the nylon anchor in-hand. He fancies himself a prankster, eager to dole out tricks rather than treats on Halloween. For the senior prank, he and his buddies had released frightened sheep inside the school, while the poor ewe was dressed in likeness to our Principal, Mr. Babcock: glasses and all.

But it's not Milton.

The creature is tall and shockingly thin; it's as though its skin has been stretched over its skeleton. I can see its ribs spreading as it breathes. My eyes keep sliding away from its angular face, as though my feeble brain couldn't bear to make sense of it. Surely, seeing this monster—clear as day—means I'm losing my mind!

Suddenly, it leaps atop the dock, making the platform shudder.

I have nowhere to go. The wolf—and it *is* a wolf or, at least, wolf-like—stands between me and the shore, and, at my back, there is only open water. I open my mouth, ready to scream for help, but nothing comes out; just a gurgle, a death-rattle.

The wolf bares its teeth. Thick globules of saliva trickle down its curved, yellowing canines. It licks at its chops. The dock leans precariously as it advances toward me. The end of the platform on which I cling is now entirely out of the water. If I lose my grip on the cord, I'll slide directly into the wolf's mouth.

"Please," I blubber. "Go away, please." My hands are numb now, blood pouring from my torn palms.

The wolf's nostrils flare. It takes another step.

At the same time, I lose my grip and slide down the plywood on my stomach. Finally, I am able to scream as the rough-hewn wood tears at my clothes, my skin beneath. I collide with the wolf, and the beast flips me over onto my back, staring down at me with dark eyes. They are as depthless as the starless sky.

It drops its head to examine me, its stinking breath hot on my face.

"Please," I whimper, pushing weakly at it with my bleeding hands. "Leave me alone."

It sniffs my face, my neck, its rough tongue sliding up my cheek.

I am going to die. I wish I could go home to my mother. We've been arguing a lot lately, and I want to tell her, *I'm sorry.* I want to crawl into her bed while she listens to *Guiding Light* on the radio, let her stroke my hair with her long, painted nails.

"Mommy," I sob. "I just want my mommy."

The wolf freezes.

"I'm sorry," it says. in a croaking, albeit *human* voice.

Then, it grabs me by the front of my blouse and tosses me into the water. The chill is a shock, and I inhale water into my lungs. My chest is on fire. Thrashing, I manage to get my head above the water, grabbing for the wildly rocking dock.

The wolf is gone.

II. 1947

CHAPTER 1
(SAMUEL)

————◁◆▷————

The Greyhound coach shudders violently like a racehorse at a starting gate when it is forced to idle at a traffic light. My Styrofoam cup of coffee sloshes just before each wheezing standstill, soaking my knuckles and linen pants. I shouldn't have spent the quarter on the cup at the last station. It'll cost double to have my pants dry-cleaned.

Despite the copious amount of steam fogging the dark liquid, I take a measured sip. It's blisteringly hot with a grassy aftertaste; the beans weren't roasted properly. I pour the remainder out the window, crushing the cup in my palm. The foam splinters, littering the floorboards.

I try to stretch. But my legs are far too long, and my knees butt up against the seat in front of me. It's been only a few minutes since the last stop, but my muscles already feel inordinately tight, as though they've been tied into a double knot.

I check my watch. Surely, we are nearing Sevierville by now. We've been traveling on I-40 for a few miles already.

The landscape is starting to look familiar. Royal Paulownia trees grow along the roadside, the cloven shells of their spent fruit still clinging to the branches. If only it were springtime: the purple, semi-tubular petals of its flowers are particularly striking, and smell like vanilla and almond. Now, all I can smell is bus exhaust and the unwashed bodies of my fellow travelers.

It feels unsettling to be back in Tennessee. I left so abruptly, and the circumstances were less than ideal. In the years since, it's become akin to a no man's land in my mind, an expanse of grey mist and desiccated farmhouses in which no one lives nor dies. It was easier than confronting what I had done, who I had hurt. I wonder, as I have hundreds of times in the last twenty-two hours, whether I should have taken a bus to anywhere else. Why go home?

Without the coffee to keep me awake, I doze, my head resting against the windowpane. It buzzes pleasantly against my skin, drowning out the nearby chatter. Most of the conversations have revolved around Yogi Barra's recent 148 game streak, and what *really* happened at Roswell.

"It was a flying saucer, honest-to-God. My cousin's friend's brother saw it with his own two eyes. Well, *one* eye. He lost the other on the Western Front." My seatmate had told me earlier when I inadvertently made eye contact.

I jerk awake when the bus stops. "Sevierville!" the driver announces, pulling the lever to open the door. A breeze courses through the bus, lessening the smell of body odor somewhat. The sweat beading on my brow turns cool.

My seatmate stands and allows me to pass, leaning close while I pull my luggage from the overhead compartment. "Remember what I said," he whispers conspiratorially. "We're being *invaded*."

If only he knew what horrors truly exist! We sat beside one another for twenty-two hours, and he had no idea what I truly was. If only he was privy to my violent dreams, wherein the wolf razed the bus and murdered all the passengers trapped inside. He had a starring role, his entrails draped across the bench seats like crepe paper garlands.

When I step off the bus, I am enveloped in horrific familiarity. The Sevier County Courthouse looms far above the street, a massive three-story limestone structure with ostentatious balustrades adorning its clock tower.

The clock chimes; it's noon.

My luggage butts up against my leg as I walk, searching for a taxi to take me the remainder of the way. Thankfully, they circle the bus station like sharks smelling chum, and I flag one down with no trouble.

The Campbell residence is outside of town, just off a narrow, dirt road. It's been a dry summer—a cloud of dust flies up around the taxi, streaking the windows and obscuring my view. But it looks just as it did in my memory: a tiny ranch-style shotgun home leaning haphazardly on its crumbling foundation. I spot my mother's Hereford cow, Clarabelle, grazing near the roadside, her tail flicking gnats off her squarish haunches. There is a small herd of goats pastured there, too, and they follow the taxi down the road, bleating, butting at one another in excitement.

"You can stop here," I tell the driver when we approach the closed gate. "I'll walk the rest of the way."

He grunts in response, accepting the wad of crumpled bills I slip into his palm.

Clarabelle watches me through her long, thick lashes as I open the gate, lugging my suitcase down the driveway. She mirrors my movements on the other side of the fence, walking with her wedge-shaped head low and her heavy udders swinging. *Moo*, she grumbles.

"Good to see you too," I mutter.

"Samuel Campbell!" a voice calls from the porch, the storm door crashing upon its frame. "As I live and breathe!"

Mama.

Helen Campbell is a squat, rotund woman, wearing a short-sleeved house dress cinched tight at the waist. Her dark hair is, as usual, perfectly sculpted into waves, pinned away from her oval face. Her hair has always been her crown, her pride and joy. She used to dream of being a Vidal Sassoon model in London before becoming a farmwife.

When I mount the creaky porch steps, I find that her hair is more grey than I remembered, especially at the roots. Her ears are somewhat pointed, covered in agouti-colored fuzz reminiscent of her wolf pelt. It's a shock. While she's in her late sixties now, she looks much older. Farm life does that to a person.

"Hey, Ma," I croon, wrapping my arms around her.

"You didn't tell me you were comin'," she scolds, her voice muffled against my chest.

"It was spur of the moment," I reply, kissing the whorl of silver on the crown of her head. A pang of guilt courses through me, turning my stomach. It was selfish to leave Wharton when the pack was in turmoil, but it was for the best, wasn't it?

"Come inside," Helen urges, taking my arm. "You're just in time for lunch." It smells strongly of basil and fresh bread in the airy kitchen, and I spot a pot of soup simmering on the burner.

"You're so thin," she laments, lifting the lid off the pot and giving the rust-colored soup a stir. The smell of tomato—acidic and summery—fills the room, and I inhale deeply.

"It's been a hard few years," I admit, sitting at the kitchen table. I push aside a pile of bills, noting the PAST DUE stamp adorning the majority. "How has everything been?"

My mother stands on tiptoes and retrieves a shallow bowl from the cupboard, ladling soup inside. Then, she cuts a thick wedge of bread, balancing it on the flat rim. She places the bowl on the table in front of me, offering me a toothy grin. "Oh, you know," she replies, "we've made do. Your father has been doing his best."

I doubt that. I dip the bread into the soup, taking a bite. The crusty bread is still warm from the oven, soaking up the creamy, herby soup. "Where is he?" I ask.

"Out in the barn," she says, wiping her hands on her apron. "He's been trying to fix the tractor."

Raymond Campbell isn't particularly handy. I've never seen him holding a wrench, much less using one. It's far more likely that he's straddling the wheel well, swigging moonshine. Drinking is his job, while farming is his pastime, and he's hardly committed to the latter.

My mother steps back out on the porch, cupping her hands around her mouth. "Ray! Lunch!" She draws out the word *lunch* into a yodel, the undulating vowel bouncing across the field. She has a voice that can carry for miles.

"Where's Nance?" I ask, referring to my younger sister. She's ten years my junior, just barely in her twenties now.

"Getting her wedding dress altered," my mother replies, returning to the table to sit beside me. She raises her eyebrows at me, eyeing my still-full bowl. I'm not eating quickly enough. I swallow another spoonful of piping hot soup, scalding my tongue. "You did get my letters, didn't you?"

The letters.

I think of my small, cluttered apartment, just above the Wharton Creamery. It always smelled faintly of burnt sugar and vanilla, much like the fresh waffle cones cooling on the counter therein. I try to picture the entryway: the pile of discarded work boots, the unbalanced, three-legged stool on which I'd placed my keys and whatever was in the mailbox downstairs. In the last few weeks, the pile of mail had grown so high that it had tumbled onto the carpet, crinkling beneath my feet whenever I walked past. Most were bills, or missives from pals still in the Navy, but some had my mother's crabbed handwriting on the envelope. I stopped opening it—there was no point. As soon as the first body was found in the dunes, I knew my time in Wharton was finite.

"No," I reply huskily, a bit of half-chewed bread clogging my throat.

"Nancy is marrying the Hogarth boy," she says. I guffaw, thinking of the snot-nosed kid who could barely hold an ax, let alone swing it. "He's in the Army now," my mother elucidates, "and he's practically running the Hogarth farm now that he's back from overseas." She's clearly proud of the match.

The screen door swings open, crashing back into its frame. My father skulks in, smelling strongly of motor oil and liquor. He hesitates when he notices me, a scowl adorning his sun-reddened face. "Well, if it isn't the prodigal son," he spits. He's aged too, his wolfish pelt adorning his lower jaw like a beard.

"Isn't it lovely?" Helen exclaims, beaming at me, seemingly unaware of Raymond's sharp tone; nothing will rattle her excitement.

"Samuel should be in Norfolk scrubbing the latrine in a warship, not here, eating *my* lunch." He practically falls into a chair, resting his elbows on the tabletop. There's a thick smear of black oil on his forearm.

Helen rises to make him a bowl, cutting an extra-thick slice of bread. "There's plenty," she admonishes him. After setting the meal before him, she rests a hand on the back of his neck. I understand the gesture: *settle*.

"I'm moving back to town," I say, trying to ignore his dangling bait before me. He's angling for a confrontation, as is his nature. When I wrote to tell them how I had washed out of Basic Training due to injury, he made sure to personally write, explaining his disappointment: *You failed being a farmer and a squidy, what are you gonna fail at next?* His block letters butted against each other, seeping into the margins.

"Tired of cleaning pools for tourists?" he sneers, a dribble of soup edging down his bristly chin. It looks like blood, and I have to look away. His grin deepens; he thinks he's struck a nerve.

"It was just time to move on," I reply coolly. "Could I stay for a while, 'til I get my bearings?"

My father drops his spoon into his bowl, the metal clattering against the etched porcelain. His mustache bunches as he purses his lips, pretending to think it through. He'll say yes, because the promise of free labor will eclipse the irritation of having me around.

"If you pull y'er weight, sure," he finally drawls.

Later, my mother leads me to the back of the house. My room is just as I had left it: bare, save for a smartly made bed and dresser. The light is burnt out. Helen flips the switch several times, as if she can coax the overhanging bulb to behave. Not to be deterred, she parts the curtains, letting sunlight in. Dust motes dance within the beam. "You can stay as long as you'd like, son," she says, cupping my face between her cool palms. "I'm happy you're here."

After she leaves, I place my suitcase on the quilted bedspread, releasing the latch with my calloused thumbs. Inside, I'd haphazardly tossed all of my clothes, most now wrinkled. The only item I had packed with care is a small leatherbound book I had wrapped in a pair of coveralls.

Chapter 1 (Samuel)

I slip the book beneath the thin mattress, my own telltale heart. I haven't written in it since I stopped hunting, and I have no intention of starting now.

CHAPTER 2
(NADIA)

———◁◆▷———

"Miss Montanari?" The restroom door opens, Frannie Lindh poking her weasel-like face through the narrow opening. "Are you alright?" Her voice is a whisper, albeit not *quite* a whisper. She wants passers-by to hear, to wonder what is transpiring in the Ridgerton Elementary School bathroom.

I stand in front of the child-sized sink, my palms on the cool linoleum. The urge to vomit has passed somewhat, and I spit a globule of thick saliva into the sink. "It must have been something I ate," I reply, turning on the faucet.

Frannie opens the door a little wider, so that I can catch a glimpse of the bulletin board behind her. It's one of my own creations: an enormous caterpillar constructed out of interlaid paper plates, sloppily decorated by my kindergarten class. "I think you frightened the children," Frannie chides, pressing her mauve lips together and clicking her tongue.

I want to tell her to get off my back.

"I'm certain they're quite alright," I reply through gritted teeth. I cup a palmful of cool water into my mouth, then check my lipstick in the mirror. It's only a bit smudged, and I wipe the excess away with my thumb. No one will notice, except busybody Frannie Lindh. She'll be talking about it for the better part of a week, I'm certain of it.

Frannie steps aside when I reach the door. "Are you sure you're alright? You look pale."

"I've got to return to my class," I reply curtly. I can feel her eyes boring into my back as I hurriedly walk down the hall to my classroom.

The door is ajar, and the children's voices tumble out, a cacophony of giggles. I glance back at the way I came, and Frannie finally concedes, stepping back into the front office. She'll probably be in the principal's office within minutes, whispering into the clamshell of his ear. *Have you heard?* I expect she talks about me a lot.

As I step into the classroom, a ball of wadded paper whizzes past my head. "Sorry, Ms. Montanari," a tiny voice chirps. The kids are still on the rug where I'd left them, my copy of *Make Way for Ducklings* laid open beside my upturned chair. But it's apparent some of them have strayed to their desks to procure paper—an impromptu game of wastebasket basketball is clearly well underway, judging by the crumpled paper balls and wads of discarded Kleenex surrounding the wastebasket beside the door.

"Put the paper away," I instruct, righting my chair. "Let's get back to our story, shall we?"

After hours, the school building is as quiet as a mausoleum. During the school day, it is bursting with discordant noise: the chattering and caterwauling of children, the scratch of pencil against paper and chalk against blackboard, and the clack-a-clack-*ching* of the typewriter in the front office. I generally don't linger after the final school bell has rung, because it can be quite frightening in the big, airless building all alone. But today, I return to my classroom.

Dimly, I hear the janitor and the rustling that accompanies his work, though the sound is quite distant. I rest my chin on my forearms, slumping atop my cluttered desk. *I'm so tired.* It's getting more and more difficult to hide it. Soon, I won't be able to, no matter how unflatteringly I dress. The roiling nausea certainly isn't helping. I wonder if I'll be fired, if my family will send me away to some Florence Crittenton home out of state to hide their shame and mine. Except, I don't feel particularly ashamed. I know that I *should*.

My ex-husband Milton Fairbanks lights a cigarette, not bothering to roll the windows down in the Oldsmobile. I wave the smoke away. "Did you hear what I said?" I ask.

He's been quiet for several minutes, just staring out at the reservoir. The water is markedly still, the only ripples caused by the slippery bodies of the Northern Cricket Frogs and Rough Green Snakes that call it home.

We are parked in our usual spot. Birds titter above, and the sound evokes mocking laughter. Silly girl, *they chuckle,* you thought he would be happy?

I reach out and touch his thigh, and his skin jumps beneath my palm.

"We can't have a baby," *he finally says.* "You need to get rid of it."

Despite the stagnant heat building in the parked car, a chill trickles down my spine. I rub the gooseflesh sprouting on my arms. I don't know what I expected, but it wasn't that he would insist on an abortion. I think of the stories my cohorts whispered about in the teacher's lounge:

"My cousin tried to end a pregnancy by drinking turpentine," Mrs. Fontaine, a second-grade teacher, had said as casually as though she were sharing the weather report. "It nearly killed her, and she had to spend a week in a septic abortion ward."

"I heard there's a place in town that you can get one. There's a woman who stands on the corner of Plymouth Street. If you give her five hundred bucks, she'll blindfold you and drive you there," Nurse Emerson added. "Though, you didn't hear that from me."

"I knew a girl who fell down the stairs—on purpose," Wendy Applewhite said. She leaned close when the principal wandered into the room, so that only those at the table could hear. "She broke her neck, and she gave birth three months later with her neck still in a brace."

"You need to get rid of it," Milton repeats, his tone flat. It's apparent he thinks this is my responsibility,

my problem. He's washing his hands of it. Just like he washed his hands of me.

"We could—we could get remarried," I say, my words tumbling over one another. He flinches as though I've just lobbed a hand grenade at him. "We've talked about it, haven't we?"

"Aw, Nadia," he groans, running his hands through his coiffed hair, loosening the mousse; errant chestnut strands fall upon his brow. It reminds me of how it looks after sex, when we're just a tangle of limbs, slippery with sweat. That was when he'd said it, his voice a sleepy murmur against my neck, "It was a mistake to ever leave." His warm breath branded the words on my flesh.

"Didn't you mean it?" I ask. My skin feels inordinately hot. I feel as though I can't breathe; the air is too thick. I reach blindly for the window crank, intending to let in a breeze. But it's as though my fingers are stuffed with sawdust, devoid of musculature and bone. I can't turn it.

"It was in the heat of the moment," Milton finally says, meeting my eyes. He is looking at me in the same way one looks at a mangy, stray dog scavenging for a handout: a blend of contempt and pity. "I can't be liable for everything I say after you do that thing with your mouth."

The janitor interrupts my reverie, pushing his enormous, wheeled trash receptacle before him. Abruptly, I sit up straight and pretend to scribble on a piece of loose paper. A lone, angry tear leaks from my eye, sliding down my cheek. I wipe it away with my knuckle.

"Pardon me, ma'am," the janitor says, his voice imbued with the twang of Appalachia. "I'll be out'a y'er hair in a jiffy." He reaches for the small wastebasket, dumping its contents into his receptacle.

He hums to himself. I recognize the song: it's "Prisoner of Love".

"'I need no shackles to remind me, I'm just a prisoner of love," I mutter under my breath. I press my palms against my burgeoning belly. *I'm starting to feel much like a prisoner, myself.*

"What was that, ma'am?" the janitor asks, still holding the now-empty wastebasket aloft.

"Nothing," I say. "Nothing at all."

CHAPTER 3
(SAMUEL)

◁◆▷

"Up and at 'em," my father bellows, throwing open my bedroom door without so much as a knock. He is gone before I open my eyes, and for a moment, I convince myself he was just a phantasm, a memory of years past. But then, I remember where I am. *Home*.

With a sigh, I throw my legs over the side of the bed. Reaching blindly for the pants I draped upon the footboard the night before, I pull them up my legs. It's dark in my room, and when I glance out the window, there isn't a hint of daylight upon the horizon.

It's probably 3 a.m. or thereabouts.

Such is farm life.

I walk down the dimly lit hall, passing a wall of photographs. There's my parents' grainy, black-and-white wedding photo, both standing before the wooden doors of Alder Branch Baptist. There is also a photo of Nancy and I, posing with Clarabelle. I'm fifteen, holding the cow's halter by the cheek piece, and Nancy is five, sitting astride her broad back. I'm gangly and pimply, scowling. Conversely, Nancy is beaming, her head tilted just enough to make her pigtails look off-kilter.

I expect to find the kitchen empty, but a young woman is sitting at the table, eating a bowl of Rice Krispies. "Good morning!" she mumbles, her mouth full. She's wearing a pair of too-large overalls, her hair piled atop her head in a messy topknot.

"Nance," I reply warmly. I retrieve a spoon and bowl from the cupboard, sitting in the chair beside hers, just as we had as children. She pushes the box of cereal in my direction, tapping the glass bottle of milk with her spoon.

The last time I saw her, she was a child. Nancy has grown like a weed in the years since, and all the baby fat has left her face. She now has the same sharp cheekbones as I do, still decorated with the innumerable freckles our mother called "Angel kisses." They've darkened in the sun, and they make her appear dappled like an Appaloosa.

"Mama said you were here. Sorry I missed you yesterday. The dress alterations took *ages.*" Her thin shoulders slump, and she turns her attention back to her bowl, spooning some of the snap, crackle, and pop into her mouth. It's as though the mere memory has exhausted her.

"You're really getting married to Eric Hogarth?" I ask incredulously, pouring cereal into my bowl.

"He's a good man—a good wolf," she says coolly.

"A man?" I scoff. "He's a child."

"He's *nineteen*, and he actually made it through Basic, unlike a certain *somebody*." The barb makes me

17

wince, just as she intended. Nancy abruptly rises, dropping her half-finished bowl into the sink with a clatter. "You know, this town has been really quiet without you." There's an accusation therein I can't quite make sense of. Or rather, one that I would like to ignore.

The milk pitcher is cool in my hands, and I pour a generous splash into my bowl. Nancy leans against the counter, her fingers tapping an anxious melody against the Formica. She avoids my eyes, looking out the window at the dark yard.

"I'm sorry," I murmur. "It just didn't feel right to come home until now."

"Because of Basic, or because of what happened?" she asks.

I put down my spoon, the Rice Krispies in my mouth turning to ash. Nancy *remembers*. I had assumed—*hoped*—she had thought it was a dream.

Laughter contorts Marnie Green's entire body. She tosses her head back when she guffaws, wrapping her arms around her stomach as though it hurts. Even the tiniest giggle is accompanied by a toss of hair or a flapping hand. When I make her laugh in the front seat of my father's rusty Ford truck, her cheeks burn pink, and she slaps her knees.

"You're a card!" she chortles. Her smile is infectious, and I grin too. I almost forget that the cabin of the truck smells strongly of chicken feed, loose kernels rolling around the floorboards. I had been embarrassed when she first slid into the passenger seat, uttering a bevy of apologies.

"Today was great," I remark because it genuinely was. We ate sloppy burgers at The Dairy Queen and sat in the back row at the movie theater with a greasy bag of popcorn, whispering as Humphrey Bogart attempted to discover 'whodunit' in The Maltese Falcon. *I nearly made it through the entire date without giving into temptation, but now, we're parked at the reservoir.*

Her smell—so purely human, fleshy and savory—hounded me doggedly all day. I've tried so hard to be temperate, to think like a man rather than acting like a wolf. When our hands had inadvertently touched inside the popcorn bag, I tried very hard to think of holding it, rather than sucking the buttery, slippery meat off the bone.

But now, we're at the reservoir, alone. Very few cars venture onto the narrow, dirt roads at this hour, unless they're looking for peace and quiet too. We passed a car a quarter mile back, its windows foggy and the engine still running, and we did what anyone else would do: we continued on our way.

That's the rule out here. Leave well enough alone.

Even the Sheriff steers clear, unless a parent calls the station looking for a teen that was expected home hours ago.

Most of the kids in town—and many from the nearby towns of Ridgerton and Knoxville too—make the pilgrimage to the Red Lynx Reservoir. It's named after the rare forest-bobcat sightings surrounding the manmade lake. It's a place known for loss, especially of one's innocence. I lost my virginity and my humanity here. Somewhere, on the lakebed, is a body wrapped in burlap and weighed down with river rock, and if we don't leave now, Marnie Green will lay beside them.

Marnie scoots closer, throwing one leg over the gear shift. Her skirt edges up her thigh, revealing more of her milky flesh. She doesn't tug at the hem, leaving it for me to see. "I really want to kiss you," she says.

I want to tell her, "I have to take you home." I can easily muster an excuse. But then, her lips press against mine, and her palm alights upon my chest. Can she feel my heart hammering?

I cup the back of her neck, urging her closer.

Marnie straddles my lap, her butt hitting the steering wheel. Beep, *complains the truck. "Oops," she giggles.*

I kiss her neck, finding the skin slightly damp with perspiration. I want to taste it. I want to taste her. Just one little taste.

I can stop at just one. This won't be like last time.

I drag the flat of my tongue up the side of her neck, making her spasm atop my lap. It's as though her meat has been marinating in brine, made tender and tantalizingly juicy. My mouth floods with saliva, and dimly, I feel prickling upon the nape of my neck.

Take her home, *a tiny voice squeaks, but I'm just so fucking hungry.*

It is hours before I return to the farmhouse. The truck's twin beams illuminate the darkened windows for just a moment, and the furniture appears warped. It's my imagination playing tricks, but I don't see a lamp, an armchair, or a cabinet in the dark but a looming reaper, an electric chair, a phalanx of men with torches waiting to set them alight.

I pull into the standalone garage and find the over-head light by touch. It's a single bulb, swinging like a hangman's noose, and it provides very little illumination. Still, it's apparent that I've made quite the mess. The cabin of the truck is covered in blood. It's splat-tered on the steering wheel, the windowpane: hundreds of droplets in all. There's a spigot just outside of the garage, and I fill a bucket with cool water. Somewhere in the yard, a chicken clucks, making me jump.

The windowpane and steering wheel easily wipe clean, but the upholstery is saturated, too. I scrub with shaking hands, using my nails to scrape the blood off the wool-like fabric. The blood just seems to spread, turning the sponge, my bare arms, and the water a dingy pink.

"Sammy?" Nancy stands in the doorway in her nightgown, her bare toes curling in the dirt. She's still wearing the flimsy paper crown from her birthday party earlier that day. It sits low on her brow, and she pushes it up with both hands. "What are you doing?" she asks sleepily.

I hurriedly dunk the sponge and my arms into the water bucket so that she can't see. "Nothing," I sputter. "You're supposed to be in bed, kid."

"I heard the truck," she murmurs. "Daddy is going to be mad you're home so late."

"Daddy won't know," I remind her, "unless someone tells him." My stomach feels as though it's a black hole, seconds from pulling me inside out. Nancy is a tattle-tale. Surely, she will tell.

Why couldn't I have taken Marnie home? I could have walked her to her door, then given her a chaste kiss on the cheek. But now, I'm cleaning her blood out of my father's truck, picking her gristle from my teeth, untangling her hair from my fingers.

"You have blood on you," Nancy remarks. She steps into the garage, resting her hand on the truck's tailgate. If she gets much closer, she will be able to see the inside of the truck's cabin—the mess I've made.

"—go back to bed, kid," I interrupt. "I hit a deer, alright? I'm cleaning it up before Dad sees because he'll be pissed."

Her lips press into a thin line at the prospect. If Dad is angry, then we'll all feel the brunt of it. His rage is a MK-1 grenade, spewing shrapnel well beyond the blast zone. Once, Clarabelle kicked him, her hoof glancing off his thigh, barely leaving a bruise, and later, he upended the dinner table when his meatloaf was luke-warm. We had all went to bed with gurgling tummies.

"Okay," she reluctantly agrees, drawing spirals on the dusty tailgate with her finger.

"I'll be inside soon," I assure her. I watch as she picks her way across the lawn, avoiding a gopher hole and an errant cowpie. When she quietly steals inside the dark house, I return to my task, scrubbing the seat with vigorous strokes.

I don't make it inside until just after 2 a.m., according to the square-shaped clock mounted in the kitchen. It ticks steadily, the antithesis of my clattering heart. After killing Marnie, I was as cool as a cucumber. But now that the adrenaline has dissipated, I feel shaky and unsteady on my feet. My teeth chatter.

I head to the bathroom, stripping out of my soiled clothes. In the mirror, I find a pale man therein, rust-colored blood splatter flecked across his cheeks, smeared down his neck. I run the tap, scrubbing until my skin is clean and an angry-red. A tiny sob leaks out from between my lips, and I smack my cheek—hard. "Get it together, Campbell," I growl at my reflection. I can feel the proverbial noose tightening around my neck, and I have to throw it off.

I can't stay in Sevierville, not for one minute more. That much is clear. In the half-dark, the truck looked clean, but it's my father's pride and joy. He'll certainly notice. And everyone in town will know I was the last to see Marnie. We saw some of her friends at the Dairy Queen, and later, she waved to the Reverend sitting in the front row of the theater. I was meant to leave town in a few weeks, but perhaps, I can report to the barracks in Norfolk early.

Nancy is curled up in my bed when I enter my room. She's asleep atop the bedspread, her cheek resting upon her hands. I dress quietly, then throw my clothes into my battered train case, bought secondhand at Sevierville Thrift.

"Bye, kid," I whisper, kissing her cheek.

She stirs but doesn't wake, her eyebrows furrowing.

Outside, I walk down the long, narrow drive; the gravel crunches loudly beneath my feet. I open the gate, wincing when it squeaks upon its rusty hinges. I look back at the house, and, for a second, I think I see my sister standing on the porch, but I'm convinced it's a trick of the light.

Nancy is still staring at me. "I know you didn't hit a deer," she says. "I know you didn't."

"You don't know what you know," I counter. "You were a child."

Ray Campbell interrupts our conversation, the screen door slamming upon its frame as he growls, "The goats aren't going to milk themselves." He shoulders me aside, then washes his hands at the sink. He smells strongly of goat musk and manure. "And I need someone to walk the fence line. Clarabelle escaped again."

♦ ♦ ♦

By the time the chores are done, the sun is high in the sky, and the ground—once soft and slick with morning dew—is hard and crumbly. I sit on the porch, resting my elbows on my knees.

"Here you go, darling," my mother says, handing me a glass of ice water.

The cup is slick in my hand, condensation moistening my palm. I wipe the excess on the back of my neck, cooling my sunburnt skin.

"Thanks, Ma," I say, taking a sip. She squeezed lemon into the cup, and the citrus is both sweet and sour upon my tongue. It's a taste that I've long associated with home.

Suddenly, a car turns onto our drive, stopping before the closed gate. The tires kick up dust, causing it to rain down on the front lawn. The driver's door opens, and a familiar voice rockets across the yard, startling the chickens. "Samuel fucking Campbell, how're you doin', pally?"

The man who steps out is tall, dressed smartly in a tweed suit. He looks quite out of place on the Campbell farm and always has. Even when we were children, he'd show up to play wearing khaki trousers, suspenders, and a sweater vest. Somehow, he always left just as pristine as when he arrived.

"Rex Crenshaw," I whoop. I trot to the fence, throwing it open so he can drive through. But instead, he opens his arms, urging me into them. He smells like cologne—bergamot and orange, with an undercurrent of patchouli—but there's the pungent musk of wolf-ishness too.

He claps me on the back. "I heard my best friend was home," he says, "and I had to come see for myself. Speak of the fucking Devil."

CHAPTER 4
(NADIA)

————⬦————

"**I** brought you some tea," Maisie Randall announces, barging into my empty classroom at lunchtime. I couldn't bear to sit in the cafeteria, inhaling the scent of baked beans slathered upon overcooked beef and jellied tomato salad. Instead, I pick at a leafy salad brought from home. This morning, it had seemed palatable enough, but now, it sounds foul.

She walks with the teacup held out in front of her, as though it's an offering to a malevolent god. Even on her lunch break, she's still sporting the floral crossover apron she wears in the classroom. "It's peppermint," she explains, carefully setting it on my desk. "When I was pregnant with Ralphie, I drank gallons of this stuff."

How does she know?

Panic is an electric shock, surging through my extremities. Maisie and I aren't close, and we don't share students. She teaches home economics to the fourth and fifth graders; the kindergarteners are far too young to be trusted with sewing needles and open flames. I can't recall a time when we've spoken in the teacher's lounge either. She's ten years my senior and isn't interested in catty gossip with the younger teachers.

"I don't know what you're talking about," I stammer.

"You poor lamb!" Maisie exclaims, pulling a chair up to my desk and sitting. She surveys me with bright hazel eyes, her painted lips pursed. "I've had *six* babies. I'm in the know. Besides, I don't have to be a gumshoe to see how miserable you've been lately."

"You've got it wrong."

Maisie rests her hand on mine. "Nadia, drink the tea. I'm not here to judge you, and I won't say a word to any of those harpies in the lounge." Her hand is soft and cool, just like my mother's was when she would rest it upon my feverish forehead.

Hesitantly, I pick up the mug and take a sip. The peppermint taste is mild, and it goes down as easily as water. The warmth of it pleasantly spreads through my core.

Maisie smiles.

"Thank you," I finally say, cupping the mug in my hands. The steam wafts over my face, and I inhale the sharp, cool scent. It reminds me of Christmastime. "I've only known for a few weeks."

It feels good to say the words aloud, and the older woman has such kind eyes.

"Does the father know?" she asks. "If you don't mind my asking."

"He knows. He doesn't care." I haven't seen hide nor hair of Milton since I'd told him. He had promised to call but hadn't. Late at night, I've toyed with the idea of driving to his apartment, ringing the bell until he's forced to look into my eyes. But, in the light of day, my bravery dissipates, and I avoid his street. "We were married—once."

Maisie doesn't seem surprised. *Of course she isn't.* The news of my divorce spread like wildfire during the spring semester. *Did you hear? Nadia's husband left her for his secretary!* I had hoped a new school year would have wiped the slate clean, but now, there's no hope of it.

"That's a shame," Maisie clucks her tongue, shaking her head; her caramel curls bounce. "And your family?"

"They don't know," I reply. I used to be a miserable liar: stammering, bursting into tears, the tale I'd weaved unraveling just as soon as I'd uttered it. But now, the words simply slip off my tongue, easy as you please. *I can't stay for breakfast; I have to catch up on grading. I can't wear that dress; I have to take it to the dry cleaner.* "They'll send me away."

"A shame," Maisie repeats. In the hall, a bell chimes; the lunch period is over, and the kids will be returning soon, reenergized. "Say, how about you come out to dinner with me tonight? I remember feeling so lost when I was pregnant with my first. I can't imagine having no one to talk to."

"Where at?" I ask, already picturing the Howard Johnson's on Hyacinth. Maisie fits in there, sipping an ice cream soda. I imagine six children—all with her olive complexion—piling into a booth, crawling over one another and scribbling on the paper menus and Formica tabletops with crayons.

The Blue Lagoon is the antithesis of HoJo's. It's a bar, located in the basement of the Ridgerton Hilton. It smells strongly of tung oil and cigar smoke, so much so, that I can smell it midway down the flight of stairs. Inside, it's quite dim, and I loiter in the doorway, attempting to gain my bearings.

A six-man jazz band performs on a small, elevated stage, nearly bumping elbows. They are playing a song I recognize—Jo Safford's "The Things We Did Last Summer"—and it makes me feel a little more at ease.

I find Maisie sitting at the bar, still wearing the puffed shoulder dress she had worn to work today, minus the apron. Despite her matronly attire, she appears entirely at ease in the speakeasy, a glass of amber liquid already in hand. Conversely, I feel very out of place: my dress is too long, my hair too unruly, and I'm far, *far* too square.

"You made it!" Maisie exclaims, raising her voice to be heard above the music.

"I've never been here before," I admit. "It's *lively*."

"Let me get you something to drink," Maisie offers. "A seltzer water with lime, perhaps?"

I nod.

While she summons the bartender, who greets her like a close friend, I give a curious gland around the small establishment. Booths line the far wall, most of them occupied by couples or groups. The mirrored bar back is shelved with bottles lined up like soldiers: Old Crow bourbon, Seagram's whiskey and gin, Don Q Puerto Rican rum, and so on. Schlitz and Pabst are on tap, the spigots spitting when the bartender pulls them. The decor is minimal with alcohol ads pasted here and there on the cement walls.

"Do you come here often?" I ask Maisie.

The older woman laughs, the corners of her eyes crinkling with mirth. "I used to—before the kids, of course. I still come every once in a while, to sow my wild oats. I used to sing on that stage." She takes a sip of her drink, leaving a bit of lipstick on the rim.

The bartender brings me my seltzer, a slice of lime bobbing amidst the carbonation, making the water appear somewhat viridescent.

"Really?" I can't quite picture Maisie with a microphone cupped between her hands, swaying in time with a ballad.

"My husband and I met here." She leans close, conspiratorially. "The silly man thinks he tamed me." Her breath smells faintly of bourbon, aromatic and spicy.

"How long have you been married?" I ask.

"Oh, ages. Eons. *Centuries*. But we aren't here to talk about me, Nadia." She swivels on her stool and looks at me head-on. Our knees touch. "We're here to talk about *you*."

I don't want to talk about myself. I feel as though I'm trapped in a mire, and thrashing will only pull me deeper. I've nearly convinced myself that not talking about it will just make the whole thing go away. "There's nothing to say," I mutter, taking a gulp of my seltzer. The bubbles tickle my nose in a truly unpleasant way.

"You can't hide this forever," she says gently.

"I'm not going to some home where they browbeat you until you give up your baby," I reply, nearly spitting out the words; they taste foul upon my tongue. "That's exactly what will happen if I tell anyone."

"Not necessarily," Maisie replies. "Are you still living at your parent's home?"

"Yes, I moved back in after the divorce." In the Montanari household, as in most, the only ticket out is a wedding ring. Turns out, a divorce reels you right back in.

"Nadia, there's no rule saying you can't live alone. You work hard and make a good salary. I used to have my own apartment before Frank and I married. Did people call me a 'spinster'? Sure. But I was *free*." She touches my hand, giving my fingers a squeeze.

"I couldn't possibly," I stammer.

"You're a brave woman," Maisie insists. "I can see that, clear as day. Let me help you." She opens her purse, pulling out a short stack of brochures for apartment buildings across the city and the nearby townships. She spreads them upon the bartop like a poker hand.

Later, when we part ways on the sidewalk, Maisie wraps her arms around me, squeezing me against her ample bosom. "We'll call around tomorrow," she assures me. "At lunchtime. Maybe we can visit a few places after the school day is over."

Maisie's stories about living in an apartment alone both dazzled and frightened me: mixing martinis at midday, just because she wanted to; walking around stark naked; and listening to whatever music she pleased. "My father hated jazz," she explained.

It sounds like such a pipe dream, unobtainable. What would my parents say? What would Milton say?

After Maisie drives away, I settle behind the wheel of my Pontiac. When I turn the key, the engine merely clicks. I try again, cranking the key as though sheer enthusiasm will change the outcome. *Click, click, click.* "Shit," I breathe.

I step back out onto the street, craning my neck to see if I can spot Maisie's wood-paneled station wagon. Perhaps she's idling at a nearby red light.

But she's long gone.

"Shit!" I repeat, kicking the car door.

The muted, hollow *thwunk* only makes me more agitated, and I kick it again, slapping my hand against the window. Hot tears spring to my eyes. The thought of being independent floats away, borne upward on the cigarette smoke of the men loitering in The Blue Lagoon's stairwell.

"You need help, miss?"

CHAPTER 5
(SAMUEL)

————◁◆▷————

"I'll get another round," Rex announces, slapping his hand on the table. He has to shout over the *blat* of the trumpet and the woody hum of the clarinet on the stage just behind us.

I watch him approach the bar, winking at a couple of women sitting there. They don't notice him, too engrossed in their conversation. The bartender refills our empty glasses with Schlitz, the foam nearly breaching the rim.

Conversation has been easy, as though the years apart hadn't opened a veritable chasm between us. Rex isn't one to delve too deeply, preferring to talk about his favorite topic: himself.

Rex returns with the glasses, folding himself into the booth. "What was I saying?" he asks.

"You were telling me about the garage," I remind him.

"Right." He takes a swig of his beer, leaving a moist splatter upon his upper lip. He doesn't bother to wipe it away. "The old Tennerman shop is for sale."

Tennerman's Garage has been an institution in Sevierville since we were boys. We used to putter around outside, bothering the mechanics with our questions. *What's your favorite car? What's the intake valve do?* The crusty men who worked there would send us on errands to get them sodas and cheeseburgers from the McDonalds across the street. Sometimes, if Old Man Tennerman was feeling particularly generous, he would let us wash the cars and fill the tires with air, earning a nickel each for a day's labor.

"What happened to Tennerman?" I ask. He was an old man, but surely he wasn't *that* old. Back then, we gazed at him through young eyes when we gave him the moniker. Anyone with a beard was positively *ancient* to us, practically one foot in the grave.

"He's retired. He's moving to Florida with his *fifth* wife," Rex answers. "So, what do you think?" He nearly bounces in his seat, as excitable as a puppy.

"Think about what?" I'm not entirely sure what he's getting at.

"Buying Tennerman's. You and me. We've always talked about it." We *had* talked about it, but we were teenagers. It feels like a lifetime ago. I've certainly lived an entire lifetime since—a bloody, painful one.

"I would have to think about it," I reply, slowly bringing my beer glass to my lips. I'm not sure what else to say, not when he's looking at me with those green eyes. They've gotten me into plenty of trouble before.

"I'm not hearing a *no*," Rex badgers.

"I'm not *saying* no, I'm saying, *let me think about it*."

Rex clinks his glass against mine, sloshing beer onto the table. "Think about it," he orders. "Sleep on it. Drink up, Sammy, then we'll go have a cigarette."

With the sun down, the night air is mild; the humidity has diminished significantly. Even in the city of Ridgerton, inundated with the hustle and bustle of traffic, I can still dimly hear the cicadas humming and the cluck of frogs living in the sewers. It's certainly not as pretty as the farm after sundown, when one can trace whole constellations in the sky.

Rex hands me a cigarette from his silver case and lights it, while I cup the flickering flame with my hands.

We lapse into the companionable silence only afforded to lifelong friends. There's a lot that remains unsaid and unasked. Rex is careful not to ask about the Navy, nor where I've been since. He also doesn't mention Marnie or those who preceded her. We had our last—and only—conversation about that the night when I had left town.

I call Rex on the kitchen phone, stepping out onto the front porch to talk. The spiral cord stretches, tangling with the knob of a cupboard and the doorframe. Even on the porch, far from my parents' bedroom, I am careful to whisper. Despite my best efforts, my voice carries across the flat landscape.

"Sammy?" he mumbles, his voice thick with sleep. I can picture him standing in the hall of his house, wearing little more than a pair of y-fronts.

"I need you to come pick me up," I say, my voice wobbly. "I need a ride to the bus station."

"What time is it?" He doesn't acknowledge my request. I can hear him stifling a yawn.

"It's late," I reply hurriedly. "Meet me at the cross-roads, alright?"

"Yeah, let me get some pants on."

I follow the cord back inside the cool house, placing the receiver on its wall-mounted cradle without bothering to say goodbye. My suitcase sits just beside the front door, and I grab it before leaving. The porch stairs creak under my boots and I wince, balancing on the precipice between the penultimate stair and the ground below.

No one in the house stirs, remaining as quiet and still as a mausoleum in a churchyard.

I continue onward. It's dark. The only light comes from the porch behind me, and it casts my long shadow across the gravel drive. My shadow's head and shoulders intermingle with the gate, making it appear as though something is lurking just beyond it.

Perhaps it's Marnie's ghost.

Stop being stupid, I admonish myself.

The crossroads is a half-mile past the gate, where Poplar and Saddle Ridge intersect. Rex isn't here yet. I look expectantly down Saddle Ridge, in the direction of the Crenshaw farmstead. A mosquito buzzes around my head, ruffling my hair. After a few agonizing minutes, twin beams of light edge above the horizon, increasing in size and intensity as the vehicle approaches.

It's Rex's Cadillac. We found it in the Sevierville junkyard last winter, spending the remaining spring months getting it to run again.

Inside, the car smells like stale cigarette smoke. "What is going on, pally?" Rex asks, his wrist draped atop the wheel. His hair is disheveled and flat on one side, probably from his pillow, while flyaways surround his head like a halo. "I was having such a nice dream before the phone rang. You remember Valerie from school? She was—"

"Did anyone see you leave?" I interrupt, tossing my train case over my shoulder and into the backseat.

"No," Rex replies. He fishes into his shirt pocket for his cigarette case and offers me one. I shake my head. I'm uneasy, and my stomach feels unsettled. He lights his own, smoke trailing out of his flared nostrils. "Why are we going to the bus station?"

"Drive and I'll tell you on the way," I urge. He acquiesces, putting the car in gear. His window is cracked, and I can dimly smell the earthy aroma of tomato plants in the nearby field. "I'm leaving Sevierville early. I fucked up—bad."

"Who'd you get pregnant?" The headlights track across a corn field as we turn onto Freemen, illuminating a scarecrow amidst the stalks. A bolt of adrenaline lances through me at the sight, and I groan, rubbing my temples.

"Worse," I mutter. "I killed someone."

Rex slams his foot against the brake pedal, and the tires throw dust into the air. My chest strikes the dashboard, knocking the breath from my lungs. "Who?" he breathes. "Jesus, Sam…"

"Marnie," I mumble. "I couldn't stop myself. The hunger—it's been unbearable. It's like when you're on a bender, and the only thing that makes you feel better

in the morning is a little hair of the dog that bit you. And Marnie, she… wasn't the first time."

"This is some jiggery pokery," Rex exclaims. "It's not a funny joke, either."

"I'm not joking," I insist. "Just please drive, Rex. Please."

But Rex just stares at me, his green eyes as unreadable as swamp water. "You know the pack rules." The pack—a conglomerate of the Campbell's, Crenshaw's, and Hogarth's—is the least of my concern. The alpha is an ancient man named Marvin Hogarth, who's wolfish form is as intimidating as a Golden Retriever puppy. He can't dole out any sort of punishment for my transgression. I am far more concerned with the police—and Old Sparky.

"Rex, just drive the fucking car," I growl. Then, in a kinder tone, "Please."

Rex presses the heels of his hands into his eye sockets, letting out a groan. "You shouldn't have asked me to help you," he moans. "This makes me an accessory. I'm too handsome for prison."

"What are brothers for?" I reply coolly. It's a low blow. He's an only child, and we've been de facto brothers since we were pups. We even slashed our palms with a rusty can and shook on it.

Rex wordlessly shifts the Cadillac into gear, and we turn onto the road that leads to Sevierville proper. We pass Tennerman's garage, McDonalds, and other monuments to our past before he pulls up to the bus station. "Get out of my car," he says without looking at me.

We don't speak again until he drives up to the Campbell Farmstead's gate over a decade later.

I take a drag from my cigarette, moving out of the doorway so that two women leaving The Blue Lagoon can get by. The younger woman offers me a wan smile as she passes, and I am struck by the sadness in her eyes. I find myself watching the two as they embrace.

"See you tomorrow," the younger woman murmurs.

"Don't worry," the older woman tells her. "You are not alone." She says it as though it's a refrain in a song; something often repeated, never losing its inherent power. The younger woman offers her the same smile before they part ways, climbing into separate cars.

Rex elbows me. "Another round?" he asks. "It's still early enough."

"Shit!" The younger woman is back on the sidewalk now, her fists clenched. Even with just the streetlights to illuminate her, the deep blush in her cheeks is apparent. Her lip trembles as she kicks at the Pontiac's front tire. It's a particularly hard kick in high heels, and she stumbles before taking aim again.

"You need help, miss?" I call, tossing the butt of my cigarette on the sidewalk, putting it out with a measured twist of my heel.

She jumps, as if she had no idea she was being observed.

City folk tend to be egoistic. They may as well be wearing blinders like carriage horses, oblivious to those around them. I dealt with patrons just like her at the Cove Motel as they sideswiped me with the luggage cart; ignored the "closed for maintenance" placards outside of the pool and complained when the chlorine burned their eyes; or when they gave me the silent treatment if I dared to speak in their presence.

"Sorry?" she asks, not comprehending.

"Your car," I clarify. "Do you need help?"

"It won't start." She gives the vehicle a sour look, crossing her arms over her small chest.

"My pal and I could take a look," I offer. "If you'd like. We know a little about cars."

"Could you?" Her face seems to ignite, a spark of hope illuminating her features. A grin softens the worry lines on her brow. "*Please!*" She's quite pretty, and it makes my stomach drop as though I've just missed a step on a staircase.

There's something else too—something familiar about her.

Focus. I pop the hood, leaning into the vehicle's innards.

Rex sidles up beside me, his cigarette dangling from the corner of his mouth. "It's got to be the battery," he says.

"Or the starter relay," I counter.

"Maybe the alternator." He looks up at the streetlights. "There's not enough light here to take a decent look, unless you've got a flashlight hidden in your ass."

"I might have one," the woman chirps, "in the car." She opens the Pontiac's driver side door and leans inside, opening the glove box. She rifles through it for a brief moment, discarding a handkerchief, a small First-Aid tin, a handful of napkins, and a pair of reading glasses much too large for her narrow face.

Then, with a quiet whoop of delight, she produces a small, handheld flashlight.

She brings it to me, and I click it on, aiming the narrow beam so that Rex can see the engine. The light flickers; the battery is dying.

"Thank you so much," she says, "I'm Nadia, by the way."

"Don't thank us yet," Rex replies. "Let me go get the Caddy—I should have jumper cables in the trunk." He flicks the butt of his cigarette into the road, then slumps down the street with his hands in his pockets. The Cadillac is two blocks east, in a parking garage manned by a sleepy-looking parking attendant.

"I'm Samuel. That was Rex," I say.

"I really can't thank you enough," Nadia says. "I should have expected this. Nothing has been going quite my way." She leans against the wheel well, smoothing imperceptible wrinkles out of her dress. The fabric is a copen blue rayon with polka dots, and it looks striking against her skin.

"I know the feeling," I grunt.

I don't know what I expected when I returned to Tennessee, but it feels no more welcoming than Wharton, just before I left. In Wharton, I had been truly innocent, but here...I'm haunted by ghosts of my own making. Every step off the bus feels like a misstep.

The Cadillac pulls up alongside Nadia's Pontiac, blocking traffic. Rex hops out, popping the hood. He has a pair of jumper cables draped around his thick neck, the alligator clips clacking against one another as he walks. I take one end from him, clamping the leads onto the positive and negative posts. Rex does the same in the Caddy.

"Get in and turn the key when I say," I instruct Nadia.

She nods wordlessly, ducking under the twining cables.

Rex gets back into his car, starting the engine. In the quiet street, it sounds inordinately loud, growling like a predator. Nadia watches me through the windscreen, her hands resting on the steering wheel. "Now!" I call out. She does as instructed, but the engine merely coughs. "Again!" I shout as Rex revs his engine.

The Pontiac finally roars to life, the engine humming. The headlights ignite. I remove the alligator clips from the leads, shutting the hood. Nada is beaming.

Rex pulls the Cadillac forward, parallel parking against the curb. "See, pally?" he says, when he emerges, shoving his keys into his pocket. "We're destined to buy Tennerman's."

I ignore him, sidling up beside Nadia's car. When I hand her the flashlight through the open window, our hands touch.

"Thank you," she says, breathy.

This close, I can smell the bouquet of her perfume: hyacinth, carnations, lily of the valley. "Drive for a half-hour before turning off the engine," I instruct. "Hopefully, it'll be good as new."

"How can I repay you and your friend?" Nadia asks.

"No need," I say easily. "It was no problem at all."

Nadia reaches into her purse, pulling out her wallet. "Let me pay for your next round," she says, pressing a handful of change into my palm.

Before I can object, Rex is beside me, sweeping the coins from my hand. "Thank you kindly." He grins. He offers her a salute and mounts the curb, heading back inside The Blue Lagoon. Dimly, I hear him shout, "What's buzzin', cousin?" at the bartender.

"I hope things start going your way," I tell Nadia.

"Me too," she says.

CHAPTER 6
(NADIA)

───── ◁◆▷ ─────

I race into the apartment's bathroom, slamming the door shut behind me. Turning both knobs on the pedestal sink, the sound of rushing water stifles my retching. I sink to my knees before the toilet, vomiting my breakfast into the porcelain bowl.

Maisie knocks on the door. "What do you think of the Art Deco tile?" she calls wryly. The tile is cut into chevrons and ziggurats in alternating black and white; it's loud, and if I'm being honest, it doesn't allay my nausea at all.

I can hear the landlord's raspy three-packs-a-day voice too, but I can only catch a few words: *beveled mirror...built-in toilet paper holder...classic fixtures.*

My stomach is empty; I couldn't possibly vomit up anything else but bile. I pull myself to my feet, scooping some of the running water into my mouth and swishing it around. I look at myself in the (beveled!) mirror, adjusting my hair. My forehead is slightly shiny with flop sweat, and I wipe it away. I fish through my purse for a bit of powder, applying it with still-shaking hands.

"Are you alright?" Maisie asks, serious now. "Do you need me to come in?"

"One moment!" I call, reapplying my lipstick. I'm dawdling now, not wanting to look into the eyes of the landlord. Surely, he won't appreciate that I've been sick in his pristine, tenant-ready bathroom.

Finally, I open the door, finding Maisie and the landlord in the living room. It's a small, dark room, furnished with a boxy chair, a firm couch, and a globular, amber-colored lamp. A fireplace is built into the wall, a poker and shovel leaning against the hearth. Heavy curtains cover the window, keeping out the daylight.

"So sorry," I say. "Please, Mr. Conrad, continue with the tour."

"The bedroom!" he says. "Right this way." He sweeps his hand down the short hallway from which I've just come. "Like the living room, it comes pre-furnished." He leads the way down the hall and into the bedroom. It's barely large enough to contain the bed with its utilitarian metal frame and a wooden dresser. Heavy curtains block the light in here, too.

Maisie has to side-step to make her way around the bed. She pulls back the curtain. "There's a lovely view of the street," she announces. "You'd be right across from a diner. Plus, the price just can't be beat."

She's right. This is the cheapest apartment we've seen thus far. It's in Sevierville, rather than Ridgerton, which reduced the rent considerably. But I'm not entirely convinced. The 20-minute drive from town to country was akin to culture shock; it's as though I stepped out of the real world and into a *Little House on the Prairie* novel. I've always lived in Ridgerton. The *honk, honk* of irritated drivers stuck in gridlock on their way to Knoxville was my lullaby. I cavorted in shopping malls, rather than cow fields.

I should say *I'll take it*. But I feel like I've been riding along in Maisie's tailwind; I haven't had a moment to plant my feet on the ground. I certainly haven't figured out how to tell my parents that I'm moving out, that soon, they'll have a grandchild. And it will be *soon*. Just this morning, I felt the first flutter of butterfly wings in my thickening belly.

"How about we get something to eat, then come back?" Maisie suggests.

The landlord turns his fedora in his hands, clearly annoyed at having to wait. "I'll be in the building until two o'clock," he finally says. "Not a minute more."

It's balmy on Franklin Street, the asphalt baking beneath our heels. But the street is quiet; a few trucks and a horse trailer pass, but they lack the celerity of the vehicles in Ridgerton. In Sevierville, there's plenty of time to get to where you're going.

We cross the street to the diner Maisie had spotted. It's an old, refurbished trolley car called, naturally, Franklin's.

Inside, Maisie points out an unoccupied booth, but I barely hear her. There's a man sitting in the booth nearest the door, and though he looks quite different in the light of day, I recognize him immediately. "Samuel? Is that you?"

The man looks up from his ham and egg sandwich. It's him, alright: dark hair, sharp cheekbones, a bristly, 5 o'clock shadow. He looks even more handsome than I remembered. He blinks, as if trying to place me in the various scenes of his life. "Nadia," he finally answers. "You're a long way from Ridgerton. How's that car running?"

"Works like a dream," I reply with a smile. "Maisie, this is the man who helped me jump my car last night."

Maisie's eyebrows intrude upon her hairline. "You didn't tell me he looked like *that*," she says, not bothering to lower her voice. "Well, *hello*, Mister?"

Samuel takes her offered hand, giving it a gentle shake. "Campbell. Samuel Campbell." His eyes flit between Maisie and I. "What're you doing out here in the sticks?"

"Looking at apartments," I reply.

"Oh yeah? Who owns the building?" He leans forward, resting his elbows on his table. "I know everyone around here. I probably know most of 'em a little too well."

"Mr. Conrad," Maisie replies. "Short little man, toupee, mustache like Clark Gable."

Samuel snickers. "Fred Conrad. I went to school with him when we were kids. He was a tattletale and a teacher's pet. Is he offering you a good rate?"

"Fifteen dollars a month," I reply.

"I bet you could talk him down to ten, assuming he takes care of his buildings the way he takes care of his toupee." Samuel grins, and I can't help but smile too.

A waitress approaches with two menus in-hand, clearly wanting us to sit. We're blocking the aisle. "Oh!" I exclaim. "We should go sit down. It was lovely—"

"May we join you, Mr. Campbell?" Maisie interrupts. Her hand circles my forearm, giving me a little tug. "We would love to get your opinion on Sevierville."

Samuel coughs into his fist, looking somewhat embarrassed. "Sure, no harm in it."

Maisie and I slide into the other side of the booth, sitting hip to hip. The waitress places laminated menus in front of us. It's one-page, front and back, with All-American fare: hamburgers, chili, baked ham, liver sausage, deviled eggs, Salisbury steak, ham and egg, Swiss cheese on rye, and various soup options.

The waitress lingers, clearly wanting us to order right away.

"I'll have what he's having," I say, gesturing at Samuel's half-eaten ham and egg. I'm not entirely sure I can stomach it, but I want the waitress to leave. She reeks of stale cigarettes and Brylcreem, and the odor is making me queasy.

"I'll have a hamburger," Maisie announces, "with a fried egg."

"Coffee?" the waitress asks, scrawling our order on a small notepad with a half-pencil. "We also have water, tea, milk, juice, Coke, and Ginger Ale."

"Just water," I manage.

Maisie orders a Coke, extra ice.

The waitress grunts before heading back into the kitchen.

"So," Samuel says, popping a slim French fry into his mouth. "Are things going your way?" His cocoa-colored eyes meet mine, a smile dimpling the corner of his lip.

"What?" I stammer, not comprehending.

"Last night. You said things weren't going your way. I was curious whether it's gotten better since."

"I suppose," I answer, drawing out the vowels. *Suppooooose*. It's not quite true, but it's true enough for this conversation. In truth, I feel somewhat off-kilter, wavering between a new life and my old one. It's a chasm with a steep drop, but one I can feasibly step over if I'm brave enough. I haven't decided whether I am. "How about you?" I counter.

He chuckles. "What about me?"

"You said things weren't going your way either," I remind him.

The waitress returns with our drinks, placing them wordlessly on the table.

"I can't complain," he replies. "After all, I'm having lunch with two beautiful women. I didn't expect that when I woke up this morning."

Heat settles in my cheeks, and I avert my eyes, taking a sip of my water. The cup is slick with condensation, and I have to hold it with two hands like a child.

Maisie chuckles. "Can you tell us about Sevierville? It's so different from Ridgerton."

"What you see is what you get." He shrugs. "Most of the people who live here have lived here their entire lives."

"Have you?" I ask, curious. He doesn't look much like a farmer. He lacks the sun-burnished skin, the thick arthritic fingertips. He's pale, and he has delicate, albeit calloused, hands.

"Most of my family has, but I've just moved back recently. I was away for ten years, working at a motel on the East Coast." He takes a bite of his sandwich, chewing slowly. After he swallows, his Adam's apple bobbing, he adds, "I think that I always knew I'd return to Tennessee eventually. It's in the blood."

Our food arrives. I take a tentative bite of a French fry. It's hot and crisp, albeit over-salted. My tongue feels as though it's tied in a knot. "I've lived in Ridgerton my entire life. I'm not sure I'll fit in," I admit.

But it's more than that. I've never lived alone. I've never woken up without my family's—or Milton's—soundtrack: dishes clattering in the kitchen sink, my father's baritone crooning along to Frank Sinatra records, my sisters' incessant squabbling over the bathroom ("*I* need to wash my hair, there's no fixing your rat face, Concetta!"), or Milton's mumbling, "Good morning, sweetheart" after the alarm clock bleats.

"A girl like you can fit in anywhere," Samuel replies smoothly. "You remind me of my friend Ama back in Virginia. She had moxie in spades. I can tell you do too." He takes a big bite of his sandwich, a tendril of cheese dangling from his lip.

"It looks like she already has a friend here in town," Maisie observes, bumping me with her shoulder. "So, what do you think Nadia? Are you signing a lease today?"

The Montanari house is loud. Mother is in the kitchen, stirring a pot of crimson sauce smelling strongly of basil and thyme. My sisters—Concetta and Angela—sit at the kitchen table, kicking one another with identical Mary Janes. They are teenagers but act like toddlers. My father sits at the head of the table, as is the custom, his eyes half-lidded; he's exhausted, having spent the entire day working at the Mill.

When Maisie dropped me off outside, she said, "Be brave."

I nod, but as I cross the threshold, I feel anything but. The signed lease agreement for the Franklin apartment is burning a hole in my dress pocket, and the lunch I ate in Sevierville is churning in my stomach.

"Nadia," my mother exclaims. "Where have you been all day?" She ladles sauce on top of plates of homemade ravioli, undoubtedly stuffed with mushrooms and ricotta. It's my father's favorite, so she likes to make it after his twelve-hour shifts.

I sit at the table, smoothing my dress over my thighs. "I was out with a work friend." I swallow the thick lump in my throat. "We went to look at apartments."

"Oh? Is she moving with her family?" my father asks. He pushes his wire-rimmed glasses up his thick nose. While he's put on a clean shirt since arriving home, his cheeks are streaked with dirt from the gristmill. It makes him look as though he has whiskers.

"No," I reply slowly. I wait for mother to finish doling out the plates before I continue. "I'm moving out—on Monday."

"Where to?" Concetta asks. "A nunnery?"

"Surely, you haven't been proposed to?" Angela asks.

Ignoring my sisters' ribbing, I continue, "I'm moving into an apartment in Sevierville. Alone."

"I'll have no daughter of mine living alone," my father grumbles. "It's not appropriate for a respectable

51

young lady." He shovels a forkful of ravioli into his mouth.

My mother is looking at me with wet eyes. Her hands clench on the tabletop, her knuckles blanching white. "Nadia," she murmurs. "What is going on?" *She knows*. A mother always knows.

"I'm pregnant," I whisper, meeting her eyes.

"*What*?" My father lurches up from the table, his chair tumbling backward with a clunk. The half-chewed ravioli jettisons from his mouth, hitting the tabletop with a wet *splat*. My sisters are, for once, silent and slack jawed. My father grasps my arm, pulling me to my feet. "Nadia, how could you do this to our family? Imagine what they'll say in church! We've already had so much *explaining* to do."

"Well, you don't need to worry. I'm moving, and I have plenty of money to pay my own way," I stammer. Looking into my father's red face, the vein in his temple jumping, I feel small. He's never looked at me with such disdain before. It's as though I've slapped him.

"Your job will fire you the moment they find out," he growls. "Then what will you do?"

"I—"

"And no landlord will let you stay if you can't make rent. You'll be homeless, sleeping in a gutter somewhere. And, for what?" His voice is akin to thunder, shaking my bones. His grip on my arm tightens. "Who's the father?"

I shake my head. "It doesn't matter who he is. This is my decision."

My mother is crying now, wailing into her apron as though someone has just died. Perhaps someone has. The daughter she thought she had is someone else entirely, isn't she?

"I saw her with Milton a few weeks ago," Concetta blurts out. "I saw them in the park, *canoodling*. I thought for sure I was seeing things, so I kept it to myself." She coolly meets my eyes. "I mean, I had to be mistaken, right? Why would you be seeing the man who *left* you?"

My father finally releases my arm, leaving behind the indentation of his fingers. "I'll call him," he says. "I'll make certain he makes an honest woman out of you."

"No," I say firmly. "I'm not remarrying Milton, and I'm certainly not giving up my baby either. I'll go pack my things, and we can talk when you've calmed down."

My father is already standing over the phone, flipping through the yellow pages for M. Fairbanks, or worse, a home for unwed mothers.

My sisters follow me down the hall to my bedroom, watching as I throw my clothes and toiletries into my suitcase. It's difficult to zip, having been broken after a camping trip during my tenure in the Girl Scouts. I wrestle with it, finally forcing it closed. Dimly, I can hear my parents talking, the words punctuated by my mother's wails.

"You're really pregnant?" Angela asks, gripping the doorjamb. Her nails are painted bright red.

I don't answer her. I pick up my suitcase and head outside through the side door, not wanting to pass through the kitchen again. "I'll call," I say over my shoulder, tossing my suitcase into the Pontiac's back-seat. But when I turn to look, my sisters are no longer following me.

The front door is closed.

CHAPTER 7
(SAMUEL)

————◁◆▷————

Clarabelle hangs her head, turning her backside toward me as I enter her stall, dragging my manure bucket and rake. Her tail lashes back and forth, whether to evade flies or express agitation I'm not entirely sure. "Don't you dare kick me, you dumb beast," I mutter, scooping an enormous cow pie into my bucket.

My sister walks into the barn, her rubber boots squelching in the muck. "Where were you all afternoon?" she asks, leaning her elbows upon the stall door. Her hair is plaited in Dutch braids, the twin tails resting upon her shoulders. Her bib overalls are only hooked on one shoulder, the other strap dangling.

"Out to lunch," I reply, not looking up from my task. "At the diner out on Franklin." Nancy and I have hardly spoken since my first morning on the farm, passing one another like two ships in the night. She isn't often home for dinner, preferring to eat with her fiancé and his family. I have a sneaking suspicion it's because she doesn't want to eat our mother's soggy Brussels sprouts, a staple at every evening meal.

Or perhaps, she's avoiding her murderer brother.

"You were gone for a while," Nancy remarks.

"Are you keeping tabs on me?" I ask, bristling. Nancy has been particularly suspicious of me since I've returned. Though, I can't really blame her for it.

"No," she replies, her nostrils flaring.

"Nance." I sigh. "I know I left under bad circumstances—*horrible* ones. But that's not me anymore. I am a changed man, a changed wolf."

"Eric says rabid wolves are always rabid, no matter what," she says, tugging at the end of her braid.

"Eric doesn't know anything about *anything*," I counter. "I've worked hard. I'm not the eighteen-year-old child who left Sevierville with blood under his fingernails."

I feel like bugs are crawling under my skin, tickling my nerve synapses with their hundreds of feet. I scratch at my flesh with my bitten nails, leaving angry gashes behind. Blood weeps from the wounds, but I'm not cognizant of it, not really. I'm only aware of the itch, the tickle, the agonizing regularity of it.

It's January, the off-season, and the Cove Motel is empty except for me. I should be manning the reception desk in the front office, but instead, I wander the grounds. I couldn't sit there anymore, listening to the radiator clang, staring at the Virginia tourism posters pasted to the cinder block walls. One, for nearby Virginia Beach, depicts a summer's day—faceless people in bathing suits traipsing through the breakers, gathering seashells in buckets, and flying kites. I nearly convinced myself that the people moved around when I looked away, whispered in tiny voices, the words just out of earshot. It was a constant chattering and didn't abate when I clapped my hands over my ears.

The air is icy, smelling faintly of coming snow. I forgot my jacket, and gooseflesh prickles my arms. My fingers quickly go numb. But I can't hear the voices out here, and the cold has lessened the creeping feeling on my skin.

"Sam?" Rafe Blanchard walks through the parking lot, the collar of his jacket pulled up around his ears. A thick, knitted scarf circles his neck. "Are you alright?" He's wearing a wool cap pulled down over his brow, a deep shadow obscuring his kind eyes.

"I'm hungry," I manage through chattering teeth. "I'm so hungry."

"Let's go into the office," Rafe suggests, resting his gloved hand on my bare arm.

I think of the poster, the faceless wraiths wandering the technicolor beach, and I shudder. "I'm going bonkers," I reply. "I'm so hungry." My voice sounds pitiable, the whine of a newborn pup unable to find his mother's milk.

"There is plenty to eat in the office." Rafe tugs on my arm. "Come on, Sam. You'll get frostbite." He tips his hat back so that I can see his eyes, his bushy brows, the widow's peak of his hairline.

"You don't understand." A sob bubbles up from my chest, bursting, soaking my face in tears. "I can't make it go away. I keep eating and eating, and it's like *chewing on plaster. I'm sorry, Rafe, I can't keep my promise, I—"*

Rafe grasps my shoulders, his thumbs pressing into the sensitive divots just beneath my clavicle. "Samuel Campbell, you listen to me; you can do this."

I wrench myself out of his grasp and run. He doesn't understand. He can't—it's beyond his comprehension. He's never eaten them, never felt the heat of it pooling in his belly, never felt a life forcibly leave the flesh as though jettisoned. I run into the center of the motel, and without realizing, I step squarely upon the covered pool's corner.

The tarp tears from its tether, and I plummet into the water, the heavy fabric wrapping me up tight like a cocoon.

I thrash, but I can't tell which way is up. I'm hyperventilating, the vinyl sticking to my face and stagnant, foul-tasting water pouring into my mouth. I'm going to die, I think, and at first, the thought makes me struggle harder, batting at the fabric, searching frantically for the light that will point me toward the surface.

Then, my body stills. The cold makes it difficult to move, but it's more than that. Death means the hunger will finally go away, that no one else will get hurt, that the ghosts of my victims will stop their incessant whispering.

I close my eyes.

Large arms encircle me, pulling me out of the frigid water. The pool cover knots around my waist and my thighs, as if unwilling to let me go. Despite its added weight, my rescuer isn't deterred, carrying me as though I weigh little more than a child's doll.

I open my eyes, looking up at Rafe's wolfish face, his fur damp.

"I'm not giving up on you," he mutters, taking me into the warm office, stripping me out of my wet clothes. Wolfish, he takes up much of the space behind the counter, and he has to sidestep to keep from bumping into the desk. He goes into his private office, returning with a change of clothes he keeps therein. With the care and patience of a parent, he dresses me, then wraps me in his coat and mine. I can't stop shivering.

"I'm sorry," I manage through numb lips.

"Samuel, look at the clock," he says through wolfish lips and teeth, his voice glottal. "It's midnight. You've made it through another day. You have nothing to be sorry for."

"For a long time," I say, sitting cross-legged on a hay bale, picking at the blades with nervous fingers. "It was day-by-day." I show her my forearms, the white keloids left from compulsive scratching and picking.

"And now?" Nancy asks, leaning against Clarabelle's stall door, scratching the brown-and-white bovine behind her fan-shaped ears.

"Now." I sigh. "I'm just trying to live with myself and what I've done." I haven't been close to anyone, neither wolf nor human, in years. I had nearly convinced myself I didn't want to, but—

I think of Nadia, sitting across from me at lunch this afternoon. I really would like to see her again, but I'm frightened. When she fiddled with her hair or waved a hand, I could smell her flesh, made warm by the sun streaming through a nearby window. It was like smelling my mother's home-cooking for the first time after my time away. Saliva prickled upon my hard palate, pooling upon my tongue.

"Are you happy now?" Nancy asks.

The question startles me. I'm not sure of the answer. I rest my elbows on my knees, staring at the barn's dirt floor, textured by boot and hoof prints. Clarabelle kicks at a mosquito, her hoof connecting with the wooden slats of her stall. A chicken crosses the aisle in front of me, her wattle bobbing.

"Sammy, anything else would be a waste, don't you think?" Nancy says. With that, she retrieves a saddle from the rack, offering me a tilt of her pointy chin in farewell. "Dad wants me to exercise the pony. I'd better get him tacked up before he comes looking for me."

♦ ♦ ♦

Are you happy?

The question ferrets around my brain for days after, rearing its head whenever I have a quiet moment. Thankfully, such moments are few and far between. My father keeps me busy: hauling water, cutting wood, shucking corn fresh from the stalk, dumping flakes of hay for the goats, and walking the fence line looking for rotting boards. When I'm not working, my mother talks my ear off until I retreat to my childhood bedroom, dog-tired.

Are you happy? I muse, in the moment before my eyes grow heavy, my feet dangling off the too-short mattress. It's a question I can't quite answer. Working makes me feel fulfilled, purposeful, akin to contentment. But it's not quite happiness. That is some-thing I've felt only while rabid, my body flooded with adrenaline, pleasure centers pinging. I wonder if others feel a lesser breed of happiness and mistake it for the real thing, having never given into the impulse to kill.

"I need you to go to the feed store," Ray Campbell says, dropping an envelope of cash into my lap just after chores are done. I'm sitting on the porch in a rickety chair, beer in hand, heels up on the railing. The envelope is covered in jagged markings, that if I squint, become letters and misspelled words. He's made a list: *Chikns 40 lbs, Hors 100 lbs, Goats 180 lbs*.

"Now?" I ask.

"You live here, don't you?" my father asks. It's his favorite retort, a reminder of my tenuous standing here. In his eyes, I'm a disappointment and nothing will change that.

I sigh. "Sure," I say, pocketing the envelope.

It's hot in the truck, and I roll down the windows. A cool breeze ruffles my hair as I creep through the gate my father opens for me. He waves me away as though shooing me. "Yeah, yeah," I mutter. "I'm going."

Sevierville has fewer residents than Wharton, spread out over a greater area. On the farm, I often forget that anyone else exists. It is an island unto itself, surrounded by a veritable ocean of fields. Going into town is akin to culture shock.

Many people congregate on church lawns, dressed in their Sunday best. They look like birds of paradise, flapping their wings to attract attention. Some wave at my father's truck as I pass, mistaking me for him. Still, I wave back.

With most at church or tending their farmsteads, the feed 'n seed store is mostly empty. It only takes me a few minutes to find the grain for the livestock, and with a sales associate's help, I heave the heavy bags into the back of the pickup. By the time I am done, I'm covered in a thin layer of sweat, and smell strongly of wheat and jute.

When I was a teenager, there used to be a soda fountain called Willy's just around the corner. When Rex and I were sent on errands in-town, we would sneak in for a malt. Or, rather, we flirted with the giggling girls manning the counter. The malts were just a bonus.

Curious, I take a short walk around the building. Is it still there? *Yes!* There's a new sign out front—it's a Whelan's Drug Store now—but, inside, it looks much the same, down to the peaked caps worn by the soda jerks. It's fairly crowded, most of the stools taken up by chatty teenagers dressed in their flashiest clothes. In my flannel button down, stained Levi jeans, and manure-stained boots, I look very out of place. Never mind being at least ten years their senior.

"We keep running into one another," a familiar voice says, and I turn to see Nadia perched on a stool. She's wearing a pair of high-waisted slacks and a blouse, tied in a knot just about her waistband. Her hair is piled atop her head, stiff with mousse. She purses her lips around the straw of a chocolate milkshake, topped with whipped cream, her hands cupped around the tapered glass.

"Seems so," I drawl, trying not to sound too enthusiastic, though my heart is hammering. She smells so good, and it gives me an uneasy feeling in the pit of my stomach. "So, are you living in town now?"

"Just moved in," she says. "I needed a break from unpacking."

The soda jerk sidles over, resting her palms on the linoleum counter. "What can I get you?" she asks. Her lipstick is a startling red.

"I'll have a malt," I reply. "No whipped cream."

When she steps away to make my treat, Nadia raises her well-manicured eyebrows. "Not a fan of whipped cream?"

I lean close as though we are sharing a secret. "If you order without, they usually give you a bit more malt."

Nadia laughs. "I'll keep that in mind."

I sit on the empty stool beside her, my knees butting up against the counter. I catch a whiff of my shirt collar and wrinkle my nose. I certainly don't smell nice, especially not nice enough to sit next to a beautiful woman. "Do you need any help carrying boxes?" I ask.

"You're sweet. But it was only a few boxes. A neighbor helped me get them in when they saw me struggling and took pity on me." She smiles, fiddling with the straw in her shake, giving it a stir. "He acted so strange, like I was a sideshow oddity."

"In his eyes, you *are*. I mean, seeing a woman living alone is odd. That's not all that common in Sevierville." My malt arrives, and I take a sip, grateful for something to do with my hands. I feel as though my words are spilling all over each other, a muddle.

Nadia frowns. "It's pretty unheard of in Ridgerton, too. My parents aren't happy with me."

"Why did you move out?" I ask. "Unless that's too forward. I spend all day with a flock of stupid goats. I've already forgotten how to have a normal, human conversation."

She chuckles. "I just...couldn't stay. Have you ever felt like you just needed to run away?"

Suddenly, I am back in the dark garage, scrubbing blood off the truck's upholstery with a brush, pink water dribbling down my elbows. I'm crying, heaving sobs, making it difficult to breathe. Snot pours out of my nostrils, and when I wipe it away, I leave a smear of blood behind. *I'm sorry, I'm sorry, I'm sorry*, I weep. "I know that feeling well," I reply.

"Then you understand," Nadia says. "Sometimes, you just need to take a step away and breathe. Though, I'll admit, it already feels a bit lonely. My parents' house is always noisy—I have two sisters; they're sixteen, so you can imagine—and I'm a kindergarten teacher too. Quiet always makes me think something is wrong."

"You'd like living on a farm then. It's never quiet. You can always hear animals or insects, no matter the hour. I can't tell you how many times a cow has woken me up, mooing outside of my window."

She giggles at the image and leans close, butting her shoulder against mine. It's a friendly gesture, but it's the first intimate touch I've had in a long time.

I gasp softly, covering it with a strangled cough.

"I've never been to a farm," she replies as she pushes her finished milkshake away, save for the cherry. It rests in the bottom of the glass, its stem broken.

"You'll have to come see mine," I remark without thinking. I wish I could take the invitation back, swallow it whole. This is dangerous ground, land mines buried just beneath the surface.

"I'd love to. I need a break from unpacking, anyway," Nadia squeals, her hazel eyes wide. If I look closely, I can see golden flecks ringing the irises. "Can we?"

Still, despite the warning bells clanging in my skull, I don't want to hope for another chance encounter.

Even in a small town like Sevierville, we may never see one another again. I see something in her that piques my curiosity. *Things aren't going my way*, she'd said, absently blowing a strand of hair from her high forehead. It was said so casually, as though we were old friends. Despite her nonchalance, I could almost taste the sadness seeping out of her pores, bitter like poison.

"Come on," I say, slurping up the rest of my malt. The last mouthful is particularly sweet, and I savor it upon my tongue. I put a few dollars on the countertop—enough to cover both of our treats and a generous tip—then I lead her out into the sunshine. It feels much hotter after being inside the cool drugstore, and sweat prickles on my mid-back, soaking my shirt.

I open the truck door for Nadia, immediately feeling foolish. As she steps up into the cab, she grasps my arm to keep her balance. Despite the heat, her hand is still quite cool. "Sorry," I say as she settles onto the firm bench seat. "It's a mess."

Blood speckles the seats, streaking the steering wheel. I scrub and scrub, turning everything into a fuchsia smear. I stop to stumble outside, vomiting into the grass.

Nadia nudges aside a dog-eared Farmer's Almanac from 1946 with her foot. "It's cleaner than my sisters' room." She chuckles. "And mine too."

As I step around to the driver's side, I try to imagine what Nadia's room might look like. It's a welcome change from my memories, buzzing around my hindbrain like flies investigating a kill. What litters her floor? Fashion magazines, perhaps? *No, that doesn't seem quite right*. She's a teacher. Perhaps it's student artwork, gifted to her at the end of every day. Surely, she's the sort of teacher with whom children are smitten with.

I hop into the driver's seat, finding the keys behind the visor where I had stashed them. "Aren't you afraid someone will steal it?" Nadia asks.

"No." I chuckle. "Everyone knows whose truck this is."

The ride to the farm is largely quiet. Nadia peers out the window, admiring the landscape. Each new field warrants the same question: *what's planted there*. She nods when I respond, letting out a thoughtful *hmm*.

When we turn onto the long driveway, she leans so close that her nose presses against the windowpane, leaving a greasy smudge. "It's so *big*," she exclaims.

"Only twenty-two acres," I reply. "Hardly the largest farm in the county."

We pass by the field of tomato plants, then skirt alongside Clarabelle's pasture. She pays the pickup truck no heed, too engrossed in her grazing.

"A cow! My students would adore her. Their favorite book is *The Story of Ferdinand*."

The gate is open, and I drive through. Veering into the grass, I follow an indistinct trail to the barn. Tall grass swipes against the sides of the truck.

"I have to unload the back," I explain. "Then, I can show you around."

The barn is quiet, save for the creaking of rope hanging from the cupola. Most of the animals are in the pastures. I throw a bag of grain over my shoulder, grunting under the weight. Nadia follows me inside the shady interior, looking up at the rough-hewn rafters, sunbeams purled through them.

A barn swallow, startled, takes flight.

"It's beautiful," Nadia breathes.

"Really?" To me, it's just an old barn. It's been the backdrop for my entire childhood, slowly falling apart with each passing season. At one time, the hexagonal cupola stood ramrod straight atop the gambrel roof, painted a bright red; a weathervane adorned its point, reminding me of a candle on a birthday cake. But now, the cupola has caved in, as appealing as a popped blister. Most of the rafters are rotting, giving the barn a mild, mushroom-like odor that grows stronger when it's raining.

The pony—a chocolate-colored Welsh—hangs his heavy head over the stall door, nickering. "This isn't your food," I admonish him. "This is for the goats." While I take the bag into the feed room, Nadia stops to stroke the equine's velvety nose. When I return, she's scratching him behind the ears, laughing when he bumps his face against her chest. "He likes you," I say.

Nadia's dark hair has come undone from its knot, the strands curling around her face. She laughs when he flaps his lips against her hands, searching for a treat. "What's his name?"

"Claude," I reply.

"He's friendly." She giggles.

"He's *hungry*," I counter, pulling a sugar cube from my pocket and offering it to the gelding. He lips it up, his chin bristles tickling my palm. "He can be a real pain in the neck."

Nadia gives Claude a final pat on his muscular neck, trailing behind me as I fetch the next bag. She watches me heft one up, then selects a smaller one. Before I can protest, she lifts it onto her shoulder. "Lead the way," she says cheerily.

The bag is dusty and leaves a smudge on her cheek. By the time we make it down the aisle and into the dark feed room, she is huffing loudly. I throw my bag down, and she attempts to do the same. But it's too heavy, and she loses her balance, tumbling atop the burlap sacks.

Her outfit is dirty and wrinkled and her hair is a tangle, but she's laughing. I can't help but laugh too, easing down onto the pile beside her. "Are you alright?" I ask.

"I'm an awful farmhand." She chuckles.

Nadia shifts her weight, adjusting her skirt. Then suddenly, we are sitting very close. Her nose nearly brushes against mine when she turns to meet my eyes. For a long moment, we simply stare at one another.

Then, I'm touching her dirt-streaked cheek. Her smell—so much like Marnie's—fills my nostrils, and I imagine the dirt is something else entirely. *Blood*.

"Samuel," she murmurs, her voice breathy.

I shouldn't kiss her.

CHAPTER 8
(NADIA)

◁◆▷

I shouldn't kiss him.

I've already tangled my life up into a thick Gordian knot, each loop pulled so taut, there's no hope of loosening it again. Surely, this will only add another gnarl to the thread. But he's looking at me with those dark, kind eyes; an abyss I wouldn't mind falling into, even if for just a moment.

The grain room is a small cubicle, the only light seeping through the wood slats. It casts long, linear shadows across Samuel's face, breaking him apart into ribbons. I raise my hand and touch his stubbly cheek, the muscle flexing beneath my fingertips.

"I'm not good for you," he whispers. But his big, calloused mitt encircles the back of my neck before the words leave his lips entirely.

"I'm not good for you, either," I admit.

Then, his mouth is on mine. His short beard scratches my face, but I'm barely cognizant of the faint burn. His tongue probes between my lips, and he tastes faintly of the sweet, roasty malt chocolate he drank earlier. I tangle my fingers into his shaggy hair.

His mouth descends to my neck, leaving a trail of wet kisses down my jawline. Gently, he presses me back down upon the mounds of burlap, his heavy body covering mine. I run my hands over his shoulders, dragging his suspenders down his lithe arms. Samuel's breath is hot and quick on my throat.

Samuel unties the fabric belt at my waist, fumbling with the buttons that descend between my breasts. I gently nudge his hands aside, doing it myself. Samuel holds himself up on his palms, watching me. Slowly, I reveal triangles of my skin to him: the hollow of my clavicle, the freckles between my small breasts, and my stomach, not quite as flat as it had once been.

I cover my bare skin with my splayed hands, suddenly anxious. My body doesn't quite feel like it belongs to me. I've certainly started to notice that my lower abdomen puffs out, the flesh there soft like well-kneaded dough. "You're beautiful," Samuel breathes, his hands slipping beneath the gaping rayon fabric.

He undresses me, save for my stockings and silken undergarments. The burlap upon which I'm laying is rough-hewn, making my skin itchy and uncomfortable. *But I don't care*, I think as I shuck Samuel's shirt over his head. The static makes his hair crackle, sticking up like a lion's mane.

He kisses the space between my breasts, the constellation of freckles that had once made Milton remark, "At least they aren't on your face; they'd ruin it."

Tentative, his finger hooks into the cup of my bra, pulling it down to reveal my breast. His tongue on my

71

nipple makes my gasp, and I arch my back, asking for *more*. He closes his lips, giving the sensitive nub a hard suck, drawing it into an aching point. The edge of his teeth grazes against my skin.

I moan, and Samuel's body stiffens. He rears back, but I can't quite make out his expression. The sharp, linear shadows obscure his eyes, cut his lips in two. "Samuel," I whisper. "Are you alright?"

"I hurt you," he mutters. He jerks to his feet, retrieving his shirt from the hay-littered floor. His suspenders swing around his waist.

"No," I insist. "I liked it." I sit up, pulling my dress over my bare skin.

"This was a mistake," he grumbles, pulling his shirt on. "Let me take you home."

"Sam—"

"I told you...I'm not good for you," he says, looping his suspenders back over his shoulders with a *snap*. "I shouldn't have brought you here."

Wordlessly, I dress, my cheeks hot with embarrassment. Perhaps it was my body, after all. "Fine," I mutter.

When I stand, Samuel leads the way to his truck, opening the passenger door for me. I clamber in, avoiding his eyes and refusing to take his proffered hand. He drives without looking at me, his jaw tight and his knuckles blanching.

What did I do wrong?

I roll down the window, the wind whipping my hair back. The roar of it fills my ears, and it's a relief. It's better than the awkward silence, the words left unsaid. I squeeze my eyes shut, willing myself to be anywhere else. But how can I be when I can still feel his kisses on my burning skin?

Samuel must be driving fast; we reach Franklin Street and pull into the apartment's narrow parking lot within fifteen minutes. I slowly open the door, willing Samuel to say something—anything.

"I'm sorry," he murmurs.

I hesitate, my hand on the doorknob. "I really like you, Samuel," I reply, turning to look at him.

His eyes meet mine, the color of freshly tilled soil. "You can't," he replies. "*We* can't."

Tears prickle my eyes, and I turn away so that he can't see. "Good night," I snap, stepping out of the rumbling pickup. I don't look back, stomping into my building and up the narrow stairwell to apartment 2B. I am midway down the hall, glaring at the ugly floral carpet faded by thousands of footfalls before I notice someone standing beside my door.

He is long-limbed, wearing a pair of pleated slacks and a high-necked, rib-knit shirt. His dishwater blond hair is slicked back, shiny with pomade. He leans against the doorframe casually, as though he has all the time in the world to wait. "Hello, Nadia," he says.

"Milton?" I stop in my tracks.

He adjusts his wire-rimmed glasses upon his hawkish nose. "You look good."

"How did you know where I was?" I ask. I haven't heard hide nor hair from him, and I certainly haven't made an effort to give him my new address.

"Your daddy called me." He raises his eyebrows— so pale they nearly blend into his skin. "It wasn't a pleasant exchange." There's an accusation there. He's angry that his name is associated with my shame.

"I didn't tell him it was you," I whisper. "But it's obvious, isn't it? Anyone with half a brain would know the baby is yours."

"I suppose." He shrugs his shoulders. "Are you going to let me in?" He jerks his thumb at the apartment door.

"Why would I?" Seeing him has only revitalized my anger, remembering how he had swatted away my feelings, making me feel small, like a silly little girl with a crush. It was like the movie *Gaslight,* wherein Charles Boyer manipulated Ingrid Bergman, convincing her that anything untoward was a figment of her imagination.

"I want to talk, and I'd rather not do it in the hall for all of your neighbors to hear. The old woman in 3B keeps cracking open her door, peering out at me."

I can't help but chuckle. When she hears my keys slot into the lock, her door inevitably eases open. Once, I spun around, catching just a glimpse of a rheumy eye, a droopy eyelid that reminded me of a Basset Hound's. "Come in," I relent, unlocking the door.

When we are close, I can smell his piney cologne, which I had once adored.

"Holy mackerel, doll," Milton exclaims. "It's practically a hovel."

"It's not," I insist.

Milton wrinkles his nose. "There are brown water stains on the ceiling." Unabashedly, he opens the seafoam green refrigerator, finding it empty. save for a few takeout containers and a water pitcher. "You can't just eat chow mein, Nadia. That can't be good for the baby."

The baby! I press my hands against my belly. "Why do you care?"

"Well, if he's going to be a Fairbanks, I don't want him to be a weakling, do I?" He shuts the fridge.

"You told me to get rid of him!"

"And you didn't," he snarls. "Imagine my fucking surprise when I get a phone call from your father, cursing at me, *demanding* I remarry his 'good-for-nothing daughter.'"

Good for nothing.

Suddenly, I feel boxed in, claustrophobic. The air feels hot, as though I'm breathing in recycled air, more carbon dioxide than oxygen. I rush to the window, trying to open it. But it's been painted shut. I sink down onto my couch. "Is that how he sees me — is that how you see me?" I ask.

He ignores the question. "So, I'm here to make a compromise. I'll agree to marriage, to keep your family's good name intact, save you from the shame of being an unwed mother, but I want something in return." He comes to sit beside me, his long legs spread out in front of him.

It is so quiet in the room that I can hear the Rolex on his wrist ticking. I stare down at my hands, still streaked with dust from the grain bags. I think of Samuel's face as he worshipped my body with his own dirty hands.

"I don't want to be tied down, of course," he continues, unmoved by my silence. "I want to see whoever I'd like, do what I'd like."

A hollow laugh escapes me before I can rein it in. "Can I do the same?"

"Of course not," he snorts. "You'd be *my* wife."

"You'd be *my* husband," I counter. "Though." I laugh. "I am aware of how seriously you take *that* vow already, aren't I?"

Milton roughly snags my chin in his hand. His nails dig half-moons into my skin. "Do you really think you have a leg to stand on, Nadia? You're just a whore, and if you don't say 'yes,' everyone will know it. What will the parents of your students think?"

I push him away and clamber to my feet. "I want you to leave," I whisper, pointing to the front door.

"Nadia—"

"Get out of my fucking house." My voice is louder now, the command seeming to jettison out of me. I stomp to the door, swinging it open.

He gets up, kicking my unpacked boxes on the floor. Something inside shatters. "I'll give you time to think about it," he grumbles. "Maybe a little more time in this hellhole will get your head screwed on straight."

Before he leaves, he leans close, pressing his dry lips against my cheek. It is as loveless as a slap.

CHAPTER 9
(SAMUEL)

————⊲◆⊳————

I park within an all-too-familiar copse of black oak trees and sit for some time with the engine idling. I rest my elbows on the steering wheel, staring out at the still water of the reservoir. It looks much the same as it had all those years ago. Though the foliage has become more overgrown. I would need a machete to cut my way through the wild hydrangea to reach the shoreline.

A great blue heron high-steps through the shallow water, his neck bent like a shepherd's crook. He watches my truck with one yellow eye, the pupil a pinpoint. When I ease the door open, he turns away, shaking out his feathers. He snaps at something swimming beneath the diaphanous surface of the water but comes up empty-beaked.

It feels unsettling to be back. My stomach churns, bile threatening to crawl up my esophagus and soak my lap. I half-expect to see Marnie's head bobbing above the water, seaweed tangled in her hair. But there's just the heron.

I'm not entirely sure why I came. Kissing Nadia frightened me; it was the first moment of inhibition I allowed myself to have since I promised Rafe I would abstain. I had tied myself up in fetters of my own design, a series of stringent rules that kept my impulses in-check.

One of those rules: never get close to anyone. I got too close to Marnie, and she is now dead. The same was true for those who preceded her. I even avoided my own kind, preferring to keep them at arm's length. *My sobriety is too tenuous*, I thought. I would surely relapse if I gave an inch.

In the grain room, that seemed true enough.

I kiss the curve of Nadia's breast, aware of her fingertips massaging my scalp. She tugs gently at my hair, urging me onward. I find her nipple, wrapping my lips around the swollen nub. She arches her back, pressing hard into my mouth. Her skin tastes faintly of brine, and I give her nipple a gentle suck, swirling my tongue slowly around the ridged surface.

I grasp at the burlap beneath us, and suddenly, the bag bursts, a steady trickle of grain leaking onto the hay-strewn floor. My nails! They're long and thick, curved like scythes. A tickle edges up my back, cascading down my shoulders like an army of angry ants.

No! My teeth scrape against Nadia's nipple, and she gasps. I jerk away from her, hiding my half-wolfish hands behind my back. "Samuel," Nadia says, her voice thick. "Are you alright?"

I squeeze my eyes shut, focusing on my breath. I need to will the wolf away, push him back into the cave in which I sequestered him. But with every inhale, I am all the more cognizant of her scent: flesh, arousal, the bit of sweetness still lingering on her breath.

"I hurt you," I manage through gritted teeth.

"No, I liked it." Nadia adjusts her dress, and the tantalizing swathe of skin disappears. Relief pours through me.

"This was a mistake. Let me take you home." The words sound harsher than I intended, and Nadia gasps as though I've struck her. She buttons up her dress, avoiding my eyes. Her lower lip bulges, trembling. She's trying not to cry. But I'm not looking at her. When the paresthesia abates, a quick glance at my hands assures me that my nails have returned to their original state: dirty and chipped but human all the same.

The heron squawks. *Rah, rah, rah!* It's an ugly sound, reminiscent of a cat gagging on a hairball. It hops up onto the muddy bank, disappearing into the underbrush. The sun is just tucking beneath the horizon line; perhaps the bird has a nest to return to.

I am struck by how quiet it is. When I came here as a teenager, cars would rumble semi-regularly up the dirt road as soon as the sun began to set. Most were teens, like me, but some were fishermen hoping to avoid the oppressive summer heat, luring the bass with flapping minnows secured to their lines.

In fact, there were no tire tracks on the road at all before I drove up. I wonder if it is my doing.

Surely, the news of violence on Red Lynx reservoir spread. Perhaps a body bobbed ashore, discovered by a young couple rutting in the grass. Maybe I was even spotted by a passerby, wearing my fur. *A bloodthirsty wolf escaped from the Knoxville Zoo and lives in the woods!* Stories like that tend to persist for decades, don't they?

I remain beside my truck until it's past dark, staring at the water. It's as though I'm standing vigil, waiting to see if my ghosts come back to haunt me. But the water remains still, an obsidian mirror reflecting only a half-moon partially obfuscated by clouds.

"I'm sorry," I say aloud.

But the ghosts are of my own making, incapable of forgiveness.

"Isn't it just how you remembered?" Rex asks. He turns in a slow circle, sweeping his arm like a salesman showing off his wares. He's dressed like one too: pin-striped slacks, a button-down, and ostentatious red suspenders.

Tennerman's Garage is far from the idealistic playground of my memory. It reeks of spilt oil and stale cigarettes; the snack machine has been kicked in, and a very agitated bird has built a nest in the dispenser; the walls are adorned with images of scantily clad pin-ups; and someone has pissed in a waste paper basket.

"Rex," I groan, scrubbing at my face. "It's a mess."

"It just needs a little bit of work," he says.

"It needs to be burned to the ground, pally," I grumble, kicking at the rusty car lift. The whole mechanism shudders, the sound ricocheting through the warehouse-like building.

"Why are you acting so grouchy today?" He sits in a wheeled office chair, scooting himself along the cement floor. "Or rather, more than usual."

I cross my arms over my chest. Last night, I was plagued by dreams of being the wolf, hunting its prey along the banks of the reservoir. I could see her harried footprints in the mud. She didn't have the presence of mind to run through the shallows and hide her scent; I could track her easily, outrun her, too.

When I finally found her, sobbing, her small body tucked into the roots of a tree, I lunged and—

I shake my head. "I'm fine."

"C'mon, Sammy. Talk to me." Rex rests his elbows on his knees, surveying me with serious eyes.

I press my lips together, not sure what to say. *I think I'm falling for a woman, but I'm afraid I'll eat her.* It sounds absurd. "Do you remember that night in Ridgerton," I begin, "at the Blue Lagoon?"

"Sure," Rex says. He pulls out his cigarette case. His reflection in the small, mirrored surface looks warped, streaky. He offers me one, and I take it, grateful for something to do with my hands. He lights his cigarette, smoke curling out of his flared nostrils. "I remember." He tosses me the lighter.

"The woman we met there—Nadia. I've seen her around a few times, and I really like her." It's the first time I've said it aloud; it makes the feeling feel ostensibly real, almost corporeal. It thuds in my chest, in time with my heartbeat. "We've spent time together—alone."

"Hot dog!" Rex slaps at his knee. "Samuel fucking Campbell has *feelings*? I thought for sure you were incapable."

"But I *can't*, Rex. It's dangerous for her."

"Plenty of wolves love humans" Rex shrugs. "I've had my fair share."

"But you've never hurt anyone." I lean against the car lift, crossing my arms over my chest. The cigarette in my hand remains unlit, the filter slightly crushed in my fist.

Rex ashes his cigarette, grey motes dancing above the cement floor before settling. "When was the last time?"

"It's been a decade," I reply. "I've had rules for myself, to keep others safe. I kept people—wolf and human alike—at arm's length. I nearly broke that rule with Nadia, and…"

"And?"

"I nearly turned wolfish in front of her," I admit. "I started to feel off-kilter, out of control." If I am very still, I can still feel the ghost of her lips on mine. It makes me feel heady, dizzy.

"That's what love feels like, pally." Rex grins. "For everyone. Look, Sam, you certainly aren't the same wolf that left Sevierville. I can see that, plain as day. Why can't you?"

"Hello?" A voice calls, from just outside the half-raised garage door where we had entered through. It's a familiar voice, though I can't quite place it, too engrossed in my own troublesome thoughts. I am glad for the distraction; Rex is no longer paying attention to me.

"Look at those gams," Rex breathes, gesturing at the pair of bare legs and high heels standing on the asphalt. The owner of the legs shifts from foot to foot.

"Hello?" she repeats. "Are you open? My car is making a horrible sound, and I need to get to work."

Rex rises, trotting to the door and pulling it open the remainder of the way. "We're closed, doll," he drawls, tucking his thumbs into his suspenders.

I finally light my cigarette before turning to look at the visitor. I nearly swallow the filter, coughing out a plume of smoke. "Nadia?" I croak.

Her eyes grow wide when she spots me, and a pink flush spreads across her cheeks.

"Hey, I know you. You sure have a lot of car trouble," Rec chortles at his own joke. He looks between the two of us, sensing the tension. "What's goin' on? You both look like someone shit in your cereal this morning."

I glare at him.

"I should go," Nadia says hurriedly. "Do you know of another mechanic between here and Ridgerton? I'm not sure if my car will make it."

Rex nods. "Sure, there's one on the highway, but they'll charge you an arm and a leg."

"I'll make do," Nadia says shortly. Her eyes meet mine, and I am suddenly aware of a floating feeling in my chest. It's as though my heart has ceased beating, and my breath can't quite leave my lungs. I feel like a fish out of water.

"Wait," I cough. "Nadia, let me give you a ride." I trot on leaden legs out into the parking lot, touching her elbow.

"I don't need your help," she says coolly. She gets into her car, wrenching the key in the ignition. It starts, but it sounds as though the engine is chewing up the bolts and belts inside.

I lean into the open window, resting my elbows on the frame. "Please, it's the least I can do. You probably won't even make it out of the lot, much less onto the highway."

She gives me a withering look. "I'm very tired of men thinking they know what's best for me." Her eyes brim with frustrated tears, and she looks away, blinking rapidly. An errant tear steaks down her cheek, dripping off her chin.

"I'm sorry for yesterday," I murmur. "I was needlessly cruel. Please, let me make it up to you."

Nadia stares at the steering wheel, scowling. Then, she turns off the engine. "Fine. I don't want to be late. I'm already on thin ice as it is." I step away as she gets out, and follow her to my pickup, parked next to Rex's ostentatious sports car. She doesn't wait for me to open the door for her, clambering up onto the bench seat.

Rex waves at me from the garage. "Remember what I said!" he calls. *That's what love feels like, pally.*

I climb into the cab, starting the engine. Nadia is quiet as I pull out onto the street. Then, when we merge onto the busy highway, she turns to look at me. I can feel her eyes boring into the side of my face. "I thought you liked me," she says.

"I do," I insist.

"Then, what happened yesterday?"

I wish we could have this conversation anywhere else. A semi-truck leans into my lane, and I jerk the wheel, slamming the heel of my hand against the horn. When my wheels edge into the opposite lane, a little sedan swerves; the driver gives me the finger. "I haven't..." I stammer. "I haven't been with anyone in a long time. I was...frightened."

"Of me?" Nadia laughs hollowly.

"Of *me*," I correct her. "I'm not used to feeling anything, much less what I felt in the barn with you." I feel as though I'm careening too close to the truth, and that is, in itself, a scary thing. I stare at the quickly passing highway signs, praying for the Ridgerton exit to appear.

Nadia crosses her arms. "And what was that?"

The Ridgerton sign appears, and I take the exit without slowing. The tires squeal on the asphalt. "What?" I ask over the din.

"You said you felt something. What did you feel?"

I'm suddenly aware that I am sweating. Dark patches spread under my arms; my hair sticks to my forehead. I roll the window down, letting the humid air slap against my cheeks, mussing my hair. It offers little relief.

I think, suddenly, of my sister's question: *are you happy*?

No, but I *could* be. If I let myself, I could be.

Just beyond the Ridgerton sign, I pull off into the grass and gravel. The truck bumps across the terrain, and my teeth chatter. I park between the busy road and a line of trees, their spent, rotting fruit littering the ground.

"I felt like I could fall in love with you," I blurt out, looking her in the eyes.

CHAPTER 10
(NADIA)

------- ◁◆▷ -------

I am absolutely going to be late for work. But that seems like a distant problem, for an entirely different Nadia. Right now, I am transfixed by the man sitting in front of me, his oil slick eyes boring into mine. He rubs his sweaty hands on his jeans, chewing at his lip. Behind him, I can see cars and trucks whizzing by, so quickly they are little more than streaks of color. They make the ground vibrate, like the earth is thrumming, alive.

I traverse the short divide between us, scooting awkwardly on the bench seat. He leans in, and our lips connect with a painful clack of teeth behind them. We pull apart, giggling. Then, more gentle now, he encircles the back of my neck with his big hand, his lips pressing firmly against mine. I press my tongue into his hot mouth, tasting the combined bitterness of nicotine and coffee.

Samuel guides me onto his lap, his hands resting on my thighs just beneath the shucked-up hem of my A-line skirt. I wrap my arms around his neck, kissing his mouth, his stubbly cheek, the sweat-moistened skin just above his shirt collar.

I know we should stop. We are so exposed, visible to every car passing by. I imagine rubberneckers pressing their noses against the glass, trying to see what is happening behind the quickly fogging windows. I imagine a police car pulling up behind us, the agitated *tap-tap-tap* of a flashlight against the windowpane.

But I feel like a woman possessed. Let them watch.

I fumble with the button of Samuel's jeans, and he lifts his hips so I can pull them down, revealing his bulging y-fronts. He's already hard, a spot of precum wetting the fabric. I touch him gently through the cotton, making him gasp. His hands on my thighs convulse, his fingers digging painfully into the skin there. "Nadia," he breathes, his voice quavering.

I pull down his underwear, and his cock springs free. It's thick and vascular, the head glistening. I wrap my hand around it, making his eyes roll. His wandering hands find my own underwear, and he strokes me through the silk, his thumb firmly circling the most sensitive spot. "I want to be inside of you," he grasps. "Right now. Nadia, I can't wait."

I need it too. He pushes the gusset of my underwear aside, pressing his thick head against my tight entrance. With a moan, he is inside of me, and I rock my hips, drawing him ever deeper. Samuel lips press against my neck, his breath hot and fast. His teeth graze against the skin there, but when I gasp in surprise, he doesn't pull away. "Are you alright?" he asks.

"Don't stop," I pant. His cock slides deliciously against my walls, and I whimper. "Don't stop, *please.*"

He doesn't. Instead, he finds the sensitive nub between my legs again, stroking it in time with his thrusts. In seconds, I am quaking, an orgasm making me cry out.

Then, he grasps my hips tight, thrusting hard. In seconds, he orgasms, his body stiffening beneath me. It must be a trick of the light, but I swear that, for a moment, the teeth in his slack mouth are sharp and jagged.

♦ ♦ ♦

It's nearly ten o'clock when I rush into the school building. I hastily adjust the pins in my hair, hoping the rolls haven't become too frizzy. There's only so much I can blame on the humidity.

Casting a quick glance over my shoulder, I can see Samuel's pickup idling in the lot, his elbow resting on the window frame. Even from a distance, I am struck by his arms, thick like knotted rope. "I can pick you up after," he'd said just before I opened the door, "if you'd like."

I speed-walk down the corridor toward my classroom, but I am stopped by the Secretary, Frannie Lindh. It's as though she was lying in wait; she steps out of the front office and directly into my path. "Nadia," she says. "Mr. Cotton wants to see you."

"I'm late," I reply. "I can come by at lunchtime."

"We have someone covering your class. He wants to see you *now*." Her face looks pinched, and she avoids my eyes. *Something is wrong*.

"Fran," I murmur under my breath, in case the principal is lurking nearby. "Am I in trouble?"

Frannie's wide mouth gapes, which makes her look like a trout out of water. "I can't say," she mumbles, flapping her hands. "I'm sorry, Nadia, I can't say."

I sigh, stepping into the office. Frannie raises the partition for me, so I can walk behind the secretary's counter. Principal Cotton's door is shut, and I can see his silhouette behind the frosted glass bearing his name.

Frannie trails behind me. "I'm sorry," she whispers, just before my knuckles strike the oaken door. *Knock, knock.*

"Come in," the principal calls.

I ease the door open, finding him standing behind his desk. Principal Cotton is a short, squat man with a penchant for cuffed pinstriped suits. His hair is a wisp atop his pate, combed over. I imagine he thinks it looks as though he has a full head of hair, but he isn't fooling anyone.

"You wanted to see me, sir?" I ask, hovering in the doorway. "I'm sorry for being late. I had car trouble."

"Yes, Ms. Montanari, please sit. Close the door behind you." He waits for me to do as he instructs, then sits behind his own desk, steepling his fingers on the cluttered desktop.

There's a lumpy ceramic bowl that catches my attention, home to a few odds and ends: a pen missing a cap, a small handful of paper clips, and a pair of nail clippers. The bowl is painted a sunshiny yellow, *World's Best Principal '46* written just below the rim, a present from last year's art class.

I smooth my dress over my crossed legs, suddenly cognizant of the slight bulge of my midsection. The rayon fabric stretches across the bump, and it's hardly concealed by the garish ribbon tied at my waist. I feel like the principal is staring directly at it. I may as well have drawn him a map.

"There are rumors going around the school about you, Ms. Montanari," he says, "and I wanted to get to the bottom of it."

"Oh?"

"You know, most of the ladies who work here at Ridgerton Elementary stay just until they get married or start after their children are grown. We certainly don't *ever* want to compete with a woman's b-b-bio-logical calling," Principal Cotton stutters. He coughs into his fist, swiping at his suddenly moist brow. He's embarrassed.

"I don't understand," I say, clenching my fists in my lap. My nails cut half-moons into my palms.

"It's better for the students if teachers aren't preg-nant or raising young children," he continues, as though he hasn't heard me. "It's confusing for them— *embarrassing* too."

I can feel what is coming. It is as apparent as the mole on the side of his nose. "What do you mean, *sir*?"

"Imagine if a student told her friends 'my teacher swallowed a watermelon'! We would have to explain that, and naturally, the conversation would become... indecent." He's really sweating now. Pulling a hand-kerchief from his breast pocket, he pats his forehead and cheeks.

I fantasize about grabbing the *World's Best Principal '46* bowl and smashing it. Maybe, he'll have a heart attack.

"I'm not stupid, Ms. Montanari. The staff have been talking. I think it's best that we part ways before the children take notice, too."

"Oh," I say, because that's all I can manage without shouting. This is wholly unfair. I'm an excellent teacher, and my students adore me. Certainly, I can be a good teacher while being a mother, too.

But Mr. Cotton isn't quite done. "It'll save you some embarrassment too," he adds in earnest.

"Excuse me?" I sputter.

"Well, you're divorced. You aren't wearing a ring. You never bring anyone to the faculty mixers. Surely, this pregnancy isn't ideal, is it?" Principal Cotton rises, effectively dismissing me. He's said his piece; he isn't interested in mine. "You can gather your things now. The children are heading to music class."

I rise, too. I'm slow-going, anger settling in my stomach like a lead weight. "This isn't fair," I spit, errant droplets landing on his loafers.

But instead of answering, he merely cups my elbow, steering me out of my office. "Good luck, Nadia," he says before shutting the door. "You're going to need it."

Frannie walks with me to my empty classroom and watches from the doorway as I toss my belongings into a box. I am able to contain myself until I find a picture one of the students drew for me: a crude stick-drawing of two figures—one with two s-shaped swoops designating hair, the other with a round head—standing in front of a rectangular building labeled *SKOOL*.

Hot tears spring into my eyes, and I hurriedly wipe them away, lest Frannie see. Surely, she'll report the outburst to Principal Cotton, and he'll pat himself on the back for ridding the school of a hysterical woman.

Box in hand, I head to the parking lot. Samuel's truck is gone. He didn't expect to pick me up for hours. So, I set my box on the curb, sitting beside it. *I'll wait*, I think, resigning myself to bake on the asphalt. Perhaps the sun will leave my imprint on the sidewalk, and Principal Cotton will have to pass it every day on the way into this building. It's what he deserves, *the tiny prick*.

"Nadia!" Maisie rushes out of the building. "I just heard," she pants.

"News travels fast," I grumble. It's only been fifteen minutes since my firing, and the news has already reached the fourth and fifth grade wings on the far side of the building. I imagine Frannie dipping her head into classrooms, calling teachers to her with a clearing of her throat. *Ahem.* Or perhaps she simply announced it to the teacher's lounge, and those teachers spread it; studious worker bees telling the hive where the pollen is.

"Why are you still sitting out here?" Maisie sits down beside me on the curb, stretching her legs out in front of her. She's wearing dark-colored stockings under her dress, one of which has a run all the way up the calf.

"My car isn't running. I got a ride here from Samuel."

"Samuel, the handsome man from the diner?"

He is handsome, isn't he? I think of his eyes, in which I swear I could get lost if I looked too long; his large hands, calloused and rough, but as nimble as a watchmaker's; his stubbled jaw, rough against my skin, his kisses the salve that cooled my burning flesh.

My cheeks grow hot, and I slap my palms against them.

"Yes, we've been spending time together," I murmur. I don't know how else to explain it. The reality is far more carnal, but Maisie and I aren't close enough to share intimate details. Besides, a lady never kisses and tells. Though, a *lady* wouldn't be caught dead doing what he and I did this morning on the roadside.

"Does he know? About the baby?"

"No," I admit. I entertained the thought of stopping his wandering hands, evading his kisses, in order to reveal my secret shame. But I was too afraid he would stop, slipping like smoke through my fingers.

"Are you going to tell him?" Maisie asks gently.

I press my lips together, staring at the asphalt. The humidity makes it appear to shimmer, as if neither it nor I are corporal beings. Perhaps I can just float away, become vapor. Then, I won't have to answer this question.

CHAPTER 11
(SAMUEL)

— ◄◆► —

E ven after she is gone, I can smell her on my skin, my clothes. My body feels strange, as though my limbs are made of gelatin and my head is wrapped in a thick layer of cotton. It takes me halfway to Sevierville before I realize it's what serenity feels like. Even the wolf is relaxed; I can feel him just beneath the surface of my consciousness, his only desire to roll in Nadia's scent until it coats every strand of his fur.

The farm is quiet. It's mid-morning, and the chores have been done for hours. Most of the animals are grazing or dozing beneath the shade of the sycamores. Only Clarabelle acknowledges the truck, raising her head as I noisily unlatch the gate. Her big eyes are half-lidded, as if to say, *excuse me, you're interrupting my nap*.

The farm erupts into a fervor as soon as I mount the porch steps. Clarabelle bolts, running toward the barn. The goats bleat, crashing into one another. Suddenly, a gargantuan wolf walks out from behind the garage.

His fur is mostly grey, save for his long limbs which appear as though they've been dipped in oil.

He walks on his back legs, the powerful haunches bulging. Behind him, he drags a white-tailed deer by its antlers, leaving a thin trail of blood upon the grass. When he spots me, his teeth pull away from his gums in a gruesome amalgamation of a smile. "You missed the hunt," he growls in my father's raspy baritone.

"I don't hunt," I answer simply, shrugging my shoulders. Still, the smell of the deer, its meat made hot by the sun, makes my stomach growl.

"Ironic, isn't it?" He drops the young buck, and its chin strikes the earth, its pink tongue lolling out. "Considering the mess you left behind. You know, you never thanked me. I covered for you, so that you could go on and have a career."

"What are you talking about?"

"I cleaned up the truck. You did a piss poor job. I went to the reservoir and pulled that poor girl out of the water. She would have floated up eventually. You didn't even put stones in her pockets." He shakes his wedge-shaped head. If his lupine jaws were capable of it, I'm sure he would be making a *tsk-tsk* sound. *You disappoint me, Samuel.*

The thought of Marnie being pulled into my father's old rowboat makes me queasy, and I bend at the waist, my palms on my knees. "I don't understand," I gasp.

"I did what was necessary for the family—the pack. You never had the stomach for it. Or the balls." He grabs his prey, pulling it up onto the porch. Then, he sits back on his heels, tearing at the animal's flesh and stuffing it into his mouth. I have to turn away, hot bile rising up my throat. "See?" he snickers.

"Why are you telling me this?" I manage.

"Because I saw you come home with that human. I can smell her stink on you, now. You reek. You're getting dangerously close to making the same mistake again, and I'm not cleaning it up. Not again."

"I'm not going to hurt her." When I look at him, his snout is covered in blood; it drips off his chin, leaving big, wet droplets on the porch.

"Are you sure about that?" he asks.

I sit heavily on the porch stairs, dropping my head between my knees. I feel sick, the cloying smell of the deer's blood filling my sinuses. My mouth waters, and I can't determine whether it's from hunger or the urge to vomit. I spit a globule on the grass. "I think I could love her," I manage through gritted teeth.

My father cups my chin in his enormous paw, making me meet his eyes. They are a chocolate brown, surprisingly warm. "Then, son, you need to toughen up. You need to stop avoiding what scares you."

"How do I do that?" I ask.

The pack meets in the back fields, where we store the massive, circular hay bales beneath tarps. They resemble blue hills, and when the wind hits them just right, the tarps shake and bellow. As a young boy, I used to imagine a dragon slumbering beneath them, and I would tiptoe past, afraid to wake it.

It's noon, and the sun is high in the cloudless sky. By the time my father and I arrive, there are two wolves standing in the cool shadow of the bales. I recognize them immediately: Rex and his mother, Julie Crenshaw.

Julie is a diminutive, painfully thin white wolf with a silvery snout. The tip of her long, pink tongue curls between her yellowing teeth as she pants. "Samuel!" she exclaims in a surprisingly raspy voice. "It's been a long time, darling."

His mother's antithesis, Rex is a hulking mass of muscle and coal black fur. He pulls his teeth away from his gums in a smile. It's strange how his expressions still look wholly human, down to the dimple in his cheek. "Hey, pally."

My father claps his heavy paw on my shoulder, making me stumble. "Samuel is going to run with us."

Am I? I toy with the idea of ducking under his arm and speed-walking back to the farmhouse. Childishly, I want to lock myself in my room and scream through the door: *you can't tell me what to do!*

"You sure about this, Sam?" Rex asks.

I shake my head.

"If you want to be a good man, you need to be a good wolf," my father insists. "You can't fight yourself every step of the way."

"I'm doing just fine," I insist, though I can't make myself sound convincing.

"Are you?" He laughs. "Now, quit stalling. We only have a short time before your mama serves lunch." I think of the deer he left on the porch, its blood pooling. *Venison sandwiches?*

97

I look between the three wolves, feeling very small and exposed. Then, I shut my eyes tight. Listening to their asynchronous breathing, the breeze combing through the tarps, I exhale. With my breath, I release the leash I've been gripping, letting the rope feed through my fingers.

As the telltale tingle courses over my skin, I try to think calming thoughts, and naturally, I think of her. *Nadia*. In my mind's eye, she smiles, pressing her lips to mine, running her fingers through my tangled hair. We're in the truck, still in each other's arms, in no rush to adjust our clothes or continue our trek into the city.

She rests her forehead against mine and says, *I really like you, too*.

The snap of my ribs makes me cry out. I lose focus and Nadia disappears, replaced only by white hot pain. My knees dislocate, and my eyes shoot open as the ground rushes up to meet me. *Oomph*. I lay in the fescue grass as my body convulses, drool wetting my chin. It's been too long since I've transformed; I can't compartmentalize the torment, and every breath is agony.

Then, it stops. I am suddenly cognizant of the smell of hay, rich and earthy, the wet tang of rot. I can hear a cricket chirping, the sound inordinately loud in my sensitive ears.

"Come on," my father beckons, impatient.

Slowly, I clamber to my feet. My body feels unwieldy, as though my limbs are too long. The three wolves take off without a word, ducking under the fence.

I follow.

Behind the Campbell farm is a strip of forest three miles wide. If we run as the crow flies, we will find the Crenshaw's fence and their farmstead beyond. Instead, we veer left, running through wild terrain. I am inundated with scents and sounds: thick oak trees with armillaria root rot; the warbling of water in a nearby creek, the *bzz* of dragonflies skiing across the surface, and the smell of prey animals, the piquant odor of fear. They heard us coming, scattering to hidey holes, ducking into the long grass, holding their breath.

Suddenly, Julie whines, sinking down onto her belly. My father follows suit. I want to turn back. They've spotted a doe several yards ahead, drinking from the creek. My stomach clenches tight; this wasn't meant to be a hunting trip. But Rex pulls me down, concealing us beneath the underbrush. "Listen to me," he hisses. "You can do this, Sam."

I'm trembling. "Trust yourself," he adds. "I trust you."

As one being, with four synchronous hearts, we launch ourselves at the drinking animal. The deer jerks her head up, craning her neck to find the encroaching threat. Birds, nesting in the bushes, take wing, screeching. The doe bounds across the creek, crashing through the verdure.

I am the quickest, passing the others. The creek water is cool, splashing against my belly; it's a temporary respite from the heat of the day. The opposite bank is muddy, and I slip, nearly losing my balance. But I find solid ground within two more strides and catch sight of the deer's white tail within three more.

The deer veers right, leaping over a felled log covered in moss. I leap atop it, then launch myself at her, digging my nails into her thick haunches. My sudden weight makes her legs crumple beneath her, and she falls heavily. I can see the thick cord of her jugular beneath her thin skin, and I sink my teeth in, severing the vein. Blood pours into my mouth, soaking her caramel-colored fur. She cries out, and I wonder who she's calling for.

Then, suddenly, I am overcome by a long-forgotten memory:

A young girl sunbathes on the floating dock, wearing flowy, white culottes and a floral blouse. Her hair is a dark wave down her back, glossy like a piece of obsidian. A pair of short heels sit beside her; her feet are bare, soaking in the water. Her scent draws me from the woods. When I leap aboard the dock, she flops like a fish, scrabbling for a handhold. Her movements are frantic, like a deer crashing through the underbrush or a hare scampering toward its burrow. In our worst moments, we are all just prey, aren't we?

She loses her grip, sliding down the dock toward me. Then, she fights, slapping at my chest, kicking at my stomach with her bare feet. Her hazel eyes are wider than saucers, bugging out of their sockets. I open my jaws, saliva pouring in anticipation, but then, she calls out for her mother.

What would my mother think if she saw what I have been doing? Helen Campbell is such a kind soul. I don't think I could bear to see the disappointment in her eyes, nor the tears that would inevitably fall. Her heart would break.

"I'm sorry," I tell the frightened girl, tossing her onto the water. Free of her galvanic scent, I turn tail, running back into the forest.

When the other wolves converge upon the doe's prone body, I step away, breathless. I want to clap my paws over my ears, drown out the sound of her bones breaking, the wet sound of her innards pouring out onto the grass, the contented growls of the hungry wolves. Despite my disgust, I long to join them, to fill my belly with hot, succulent meat. But instead, I kneel upon the creek bed, cleaning my paws and snout in the water, then I drink until I can no longer taste copper upon my tongue.

To anchor myself there, I think of Nadia's gentle hands, her dark hair, her hazel eyes, her—

Oh god. The girl was Nadia.

CHAPTER 12
(NADIA)

————◁◆▷————

The King Street Coffee Shop and Confectionary is a half-block from Ridgerton Elementary on the same street. From the window, I'll be able to see Samuel's rusty old pickup. I wish I had his phone number, so I could call and tell him what's happened. Having to stay near the school has felt like an indignity, especially when students' parents have come in for a cup of coffee.

Every interaction is the same. First, they stare, as if trying to place me. Then, a gasp of recognition: "Ms. Montanari, what a surprise!" And I'm sure it is. Seeing a teacher outside of the school building is akin to seeing a turtle without its shell, even for parents. After pleasantries, the conversation inevitably fizzles, too mired in awkwardness. They desperately want to ask why I'm there during school hours. I desperately want to hide under my table. A student, getting a treat after a dentist appointment, is the only one who dares ask me outright. "Did you go to the dentist too?"

Finally, I see Samuel's red pickup, its tailpipe farting black smoke when he shifts gears. I trot out onto the sidewalk, waving both arms as if I've been stranded on a desert island rather than downing cup after cup of coffee. He waves.

"Nadia!" someone exclaims, the voice punctuated by the *ti-TING* of the bell above Parrish Hardware, next door to the coffee shop. *Milton.*

I slowly turn, my bowels turning to water. He's holding a paper bag with the hardware store's mascot printed on the side: a wrench with a toothy smile. "I thought that was you."

The truck pulls up to the curb. I fantasize about jumping into the cab, screaming at Samuel to *go, go, go*. But it's as though I've grown roots. I can't move. "Hello Milton," I manage, around the lump in my throat.

Milton looks past me at the idling truck. I turn to look, too. Samuel leans across the passenger seat, cranking the window down. "Are you ready to go?" he asks.

"Who's this?" Milton asks, his nostrils flaring. The paper bag crinkles in his fist.

"My ride," I reply meekly.

"Is everything alright here?" Samuel asks.

"She doesn't need bupkis from you," Milton says coolly. "Move along. *I'll* take *my* girl home." He steps closer to me, grasping my elbow with his free hand. His posturing would be laughable if I didn't feel so sick.

Samuel's dark eyes narrow. "Your girl?" he murmurs. His jaw ratchets so tight that I fear he will pulverize his molars.

I pull my arm from his grasp. "I'm not going with you, Milton." My voice sounds shrill and pitiful, and I wish I hadn't said a word. I reach for the truck's door handle, but Milton grabs my arm again, wrenching me toward him. This time, his grip is strong.

"What will people say," he says, faux sweetness dripping off of his teeth, "if the woman carrying my baby is seen riding around with a...a...country *bumpkin*."

Despite the heat, a shiver sweeps through me.

Samuel isn't looking at me, nor Milton. Instead, he stares through the front windscreen, both hands on the wheel. For a moment, I think he's simply going to drive off. But then, he opens the driver's side door, walking around the truck to mount the sidewalk. "I'm going to need you to release the lady," he growls. Standing nose-to-nose, Samuel is much larger than Milton, his body adorned with ropy muscle. Still, Milton is undeterred.

Milton laughs. "I'm going to need *you* to get back into your truck and fuck off. You aren't driving my pregnant fiancé home."

"I told you I'm not going to marry you, Milton!" I struggle to free my arm from his grasp, but it's as though it's caught in a vice. "You and I—we aren't *anything*. You made very certain of that."

Samuel's eyes glint. Suddenly, he reaches out, his big mitt grasping Milton's throat. Surprised, Milton releases me, and I skitter away, my back against the truck. Samuel's thumb presses against Milton's Adam's apple, making the smaller man gasp.

"I'm going to ask you to turn the fuck around and be on your way," Samuel snarls. His voice seems to have sunk down an octave, and it trembles with what can only be described as unbridled fury. Abruptly, he lets Milton go, pushing him back toward the storefront.

Milton coughs, spitting onto the sidewalk. He looks from Samuel to me, his mouth agape. His face is beet red.

"You should be ashamed of yourself," he rasps, glaring daggers at me. "What have you been doing in that podunk town, huh? Whoring around with the likes of *him?* I always knew you were a fucking floozy bi—"

Abruptly, Samuel grabs Milton by the hair, slamming his head into the truck door mere inches from me. Startled, I let out a strangled squeak. He pulls Milton's head back, intending to slam it into the steel frame again, but I grasp his arm in both hands. "Stop," I shout. "Sam, you'll kill him. *Stop.*"

Sam's eyes aren't his; they are a predator's eyes, depthless like the sharks I've seen in my father's *National Geographic* magazines. Then, he blinks, and I can see my reflection in them, my eyes wide and frightened. "I'm sorry," he murmurs. He releases Milton, who crumples into a heap on the sidewalk, clutching at his forehead and moaning.

"Take me home," I say, and Samuel does as I ask.

Samuel trails behind me as I unlock the apartment door. We barely spoke on the drive back to Sevierville, and when we pulled into the apartment building's lot, he nodded when I meekly asked, "Will you come in?"

"I'm sorry," I blurt out. "I should have told you." I sink down onto the nest of pillows and blankets on the couch, pulling a heavy quilt over my thin shoulders.

Samuel sits, too. With the blinds drawn, I can't quite make out his expression.

"Milton was my boyfriend," I say, "Or, I guess he wasn't. I thought he was. When I got p-p-pregnant, he wanted nothing to do with it. So, Maisie helped me get this apartment, and I planned to do this all on my own. I really thought I was going to make it work." A sob bubbles up, and I clap my hand over my mouth, embarrassed. "But it's all falling apart."

Samuel listens as I recount my family's piss-poor reaction, Milton's ultimatum, the meeting with the principal. By the time I am done, I'm bawling, wiping at my snotty nose with the quilt.

"Nadia," Samuel finally says. "I'm not angry with you." He moves closer, taking my hand in his. His knuckles are swollen, the joint of his pointer finger split. He must have hurt himself when slamming Milton's head against the truck. I run my fingers over his puffy skin. "I know what it's like to have a secret. It feels—"

He presses his lips together, trying to find the words. "It feels like you are having a funeral for yourself, and the ceremony never ends. You just keep stripping layers away, and you wonder what you'll find when you finally peel away the last one."

As he speaks, his fingers find the copper buttons of my dress, unfastening each one in turn. "What I've also learned about secrets," he continues, "is that they aren't worth keeping. Not really. Someone will still love you, even when you are laid bare."

Samuel pushes my dress off my shoulders, and the fabric pools around my waist. Then, he kisses me, his mouth hot and insistent. I'm trembling, unsure, unable to reciprocate. Surely, this is a trick. I imagine him pulling away, laughing in my face. *You really think I would care about you?*

He kisses my cheek, my jaw, his teeth grazing against my earlobe. "I don't want this to stop—you and me," he murmurs into my ear. "I want you, even if it's not *just* you." His big palm rests against my belly.

"I want you too," I murmur.

Samuel pulls my dress off my hips, tossing it aside. While I watch, eyes half-lidded, he unbuttons his jeans, peeling them off his thick legs. His cock is already hard, tenting the front of his underwear, straining against the fabric. Gentle, Samuel presses me into the couch, his body covering mine; his cock butts up against my pubic bone. I pull his shirt over his head, running my hands over his broad, muscular back. His skin twitches beneath my hands.

Like he had this morning, Samuel pulls down the cups of my bra, sucking my nipple into his mouth. His tongue swirls around the stiffening nub, making me moan and clutch at his hair. Abruptly, he releases my nipple, kissing down the curve of my stomach. Then, his fingers hook around my underwear, pulling them down my thighs.

He kisses the mound of flesh just above my most sensitive spot, then the tops of each of my thighs. He is teasing me; I can feel the curve of his grin against my flesh. I buck my hips. *Please*. But he just runs the flat of his tongue up my thigh.

"Sam," I whimper.

Finally, *finally,* he probes between my folds, pressing his lips against the pink nub tucked at their apex. He gently licks, making my body tremble violently. Within seconds, I orgasm, clasping my thighs tightly around his ears.

Samuel sits up, stroking his thick cock with one hand. His chin is wet with my desire, and he wipes it away with his free hand. I reach for his cock, replacing his hand with mine. His lips parted and eyes half-lidded, Samuel watches me as I tentatively kiss the bulbous tip. When I take him into my mouth, swirling my tongue, the sound he makes is akin to a howl.

CHAPTER 13
(SAMUEL)

———— ◁◆▷ ————

We lay naked on the couch, our limbs intertwined. Nadia nuzzles my neck, dragging her fingers through my hair. Despite my contentment, a bothersome thought buzzes around my head like a mosquito. *You have to tell her.*

I bat it away, drawing patterns on her rib cage with my fingertips.

"You don't have to stay," Nadia finally murmurs. Her voice startles me. I think I may have been dozing.

"What do you mean?" I ask sleepily.

"I'm just saying…maybe *this* was the heat of the moment. Maybe you said things you don't really mean—that you regret. I want you to know that you can still go. I won't hold you to it." She sits up so that she can meet my eyes; her hair draped over her naked shoulder.

I raise my eyebrows. "Would you like me to go?"

"No." She shakes her head. "But it's not just me, is it?"

"Nadia." I sit up. "I meant every word I said. I want to be with you, and I know that means I'm going to share you with whoever is in *here*." I rest my hand upon her abdomen, and to my surprise, I can feel something flutter against my palm, turning lazy somersaults.

Nadia's hands cover mine.

Tell her. Tell her!

"But," I say, letting the word linger on my tongue. "First, I have to tell you a secret, too."

Nadia sits up, too, pulling the throw blanket draped across the couch back around her shoulders. It's a loose knit, revealing tantalizing diamonds of her pale flesh beneath. Her eyebrows knit together, concerned.

"I'm not what you think I am," I blurt out before I lose my nerve. "In fact, I think that we met years ago, under bad circumstances. Let me show you."

She watches, wordlessly, as I hold out my hands, palms up. The skin there thickens, becoming leathery. Then, I flip them, so that she can see the pale silver fur erupting from my pores, the thick talons growing from my cuticles. She places her small hand over my paw, stroking the silky fur with trembling fingers. With effort, I halt the transformation there.

"I convinced myself it was a dream," she breathes. "Something my brain connected when I fainted, falling into the water. But it was *you*?" Her hazel eyes brim with tears, looking into my face.

"It was me," I say softly. "But not *me*. Nadia, I was sick for a long time. I hurt a lot of people, many of whom I cared about. You can't possibly understand, but that afternoon, on the dock, you reminded me of my humanity. I should have told you sooner."

Nadia rises from the couch, putting the coffee table between us. The tassels of the blanket swish around her naked thighs. Her belly is a smooth curve. "I feel as though I'm dreaming now. Is it possible to have a good and bad dream at once?"

My hands, resting in my lap, return to their normal, human state. I clench them into fists, then let them relax. "I ask myself that a lot. I feel like I'm straddling both extremes, all of the time. But, not when I'm with you. When I'm with you, everything settles into place. I have been trying very hard to be a good wolf, but you make me a good man. I'm going to prove it to you—if you'll let me."

"I need time," she says, not meeting my eyes.

EPILOGUE
(NADIA)

⊲◆⊳

Pennant banners crisscross the parking lot of Tennerman's, marking the garage's Grand Opening. The atmosphere is festive: giggling children run between popcorn and cotton candy carts, their faces painted, adults drink beer and admire a parade of vintage cars, all while Samuel and Rex stand in the thick of it.

Samuel holds my sleeping son, Henry, in the crook of his elbow, rocking her gently. Her chubby cheek rests upon his chest, leaving a spreading splotch of drool on his dress shirt. But he doesn't seem to mind. The garage's door is open, and inside, I can see my Pontiac up on the lift, their inaugural repair.

Nancy, Samuel's sister, brings me a beer. "I never thought my brother would be the domestic type," she remarks. "Fatherhood looks good on him. *You've* been good for him."

We didn't speak for several days after his startling confession. Then, he arrived at my apartment with a bag of his old baby clothes, claiming he couldn't stay.

"Rex and I are putting in an offer on the garage," he explained. A few weeks later, he helped me build a crib and dresser. When I was ready, he let me undress him, and he kissed all the spots that ached for him.

In October, when I went into labor, he refused to leave my side, despite the nurses' apparent disapproval. *Fathers usually wait outside smoking cigars*, one muttered, but he pretended not to hear her.

"Are you coming to the hunt?" Nancy asks. Every Sunday, the Campbell's and their pack go hunting, returning to the farm with venison or rabbit. Then, Helen Campbell roasts the meat, serving it alongside glazed carrots, brussel sprouts, cherry compote, radish asparagus salad, or whatever crop is in season. It's their version of a family cookout. Since the day Samuel introduced me to his family, I've been more than welcome at the table.

I nod. "I promised your dad I would bring my chocolate chip cookies." I take a sip of my beer. It's an autumnal brew with hints of apple, perfect for a beautiful late fall day. There's a slight chill in the air, but it's invigorating, not unpleasant. I find myself looking forward to tonight's festivities. Initially, I found the hunt somewhat barbaric, unaccustomed to seeing my food with its fur still on, blood dripping. But now, I crave the quiet moment on the porch after Samuel returns, when I can rest my cheek on his cool fur, inhaling the sweet smell of the outdoors.

Later, Samuel finds me in the crowd. Henry is awake now, looking around with hazel eyes, more green than brown. I take him, kissing his bald head.

"We're proud of you," I tell him, threading my fingers with his. "You're a good man, Samuel Campbell."

♦ ♦ ♦

THE END

ABOUT THE AUTHOR
BEAU LAKE

———◁◆▷———

B eau Lake is a tattooed, blue-haired, queer romance
writer skulking around the mountains of Virginia.
She is very happily married and lives with a menagerie
of children (2), dogs (3), and plants.

Her current hobbies include digital art, social/
animal activism, and screaming into the void. Mostly
the latter. She is passionate about ending greyhound
racing in the United States and worldwide, and shares
her home with a retired racer named River. Other
favorite activities include listening to true crime pod-
casts, staring at empty Word documents while having
existential crises, and asking herself "What Would
Stephen King Do?"

Beau writes both traditional and horror/supernat-
ural LGBTQIA romance. Werewolves are her favorite
because they have sharp teeth and even sharper
personalities.

Some of her published work includes the well-re-
ceived DC Pride series, co-written with Tatum West

(Proud, Out, and The Space Between Us). The Wolves of Wharton is her first supernatural series, with more to come!

She can be found online via Facebook, Twitter, or at authorbeaulake.com. She loves t3alking with readers and can be reached at authorbeaulake@gmail.com. Vegetarian recipes are also appreciated.

facebook.com/beau.lake.77
facebook.com/groups/1813967932089935
Twitter @beau__lakebeaulakebooks.com

OTHER BOOKS

Co-authored w/ Tatum West:
Proud, Out, The Space Between Us

BY BEAU LAKE:

The Beast Beside Me
The Beast Within Me

4 Horsemen Publications

Romance

Ann Shepphird
The War Council

Emily Bunney
All or Nothing
All the Way
All Night Long
All She Needs
Having it All
All at Once
All Together
All for Her

Lynn Chantale
The Baker's Touch
Blind Secrets

Mimi Francis
Private Lives
Second Chances
Run Away Home
The Professor

Fantasy & Paranormal Romance

Beau Lake
The Beast Beside Me
The Beast Within Me
The Beast After Me
The Beast Like Me
An Eye for Emeralds
Swimming in Sapphires
Pining for Pearls

D. Lambert
To Walk into the Sands
Rydan
Northlander
Esparan
King
Traitor
His Last Name

J.M. PAQUETTE
Klauden's Ring
Solyn's Body
The Inbetween
Hannah's Heart
Call Me Forth
Invite Me In

LYRE R. SAENZ
Prelude
Falsetto in the Woods
Ragtime Swing
Sonata
Song of the Sea
The Devil's Trill
Bercuese

To Heal a Songbird
Ghost March
Nocturne

VALERIE WILLIS
Cedric: The Demonic Knight
Romasanta: Father of
Werewolves
The Oracle: Keeper of the
Gaea's Gate
Artemis: Eye of Gaea
King Incubus: A New Reign

V.C. WILLIS
Prince's Priest
Priest's Assassin

YOUNG ADULT FANTASY

BLAISE RAMSAY
Through The Black Mirror
The City of Nightmares
The Astral Tower
The Lost Book of
the Old Blood
Shadow of the Dark Witch
Chamber of the Dead God

C.R. RICE
Denial
Anger
Bargaining
Depression
Acceptance
Broken Beginnings:
Story of Thane
Shattered Start: Story of Sera
Sins of The Father:
Story of Silas
Honorable Darkness: Story of
Hex and Snip
A Love Lost: Story of Radnar

4HORSEMENPUBLICATIONS.COM